Samuel Western is a two-time winner of the Wyoming Literary Fellowship. His book of poetry, *A Random Census of Souls*, was a finalist for the High Plains Book Award. His latest work of fiction, *Canyons*, was published by the Fifthian Press.

OTHER WORKS BY SAMUEL WESTERN

Pushed Off the Mountain, Sold Down the River; Wyoming's Search for its Soul (2002)

A Random Census of Souls (2009)

Canyons (2016)

The Spirit of 1889: Restoring the Promise of the High Plains and Northern Rockies (2024)

KATANA

Samuel Western

Bootleg Road Press
Sheridan, Wyoming

Copyright© 2025
All rights reserved

ISBN: 979-8-218-8760-8

For my brother, Matthew

*"As I dig for wild orchids
in the autumn fields,
it is the deeply-bedded root
that I desire, not the flower."*

                                            Izumi Shikibu

Bohdi
(Awakening)

"It's the sword, isn't it?" said Sylvia.

I pushed around a poached egg floating in a sea of reduced tomato base, a dish I usually relished. Sylvia had made the sauce from scratch, using the heritage tomatoes we tended in our backyard. Now it tasted like soup out of a can.

"That's what's bothering you. Right? Look, you've barely touched your food."

I looked out the window of our golf course condominium. A man glanced around to see if anyone was watching, then toed the golf ball out of the tall grass onto the fairway. I had forgotten the man's name, which happens a lot these days. He was a lout, a braggart who spent a lot of time at the clubhouse bar. He had owned a debt collection agency in Casper, Wyoming and likely been a manipulator all his days.

"You've got to do something," said Sylvia. "You can't go on like this, moping about."

"Doesn't being eighty earn one the right to occasionally be contemplative?" I asked.

"Contemplative, yes. Morose, no. Besides, you've been this way for a month," said Sylvia, again regarding my nearly full plate.

She was right, of course. I, in my conflict avoidant ways was relying on Sylvia, as I had for four decades, to light a fire.

The debt collector swatted gracelessly at his fudged ball. I couldn't see its flight. But by the way he stuffed his iron into his golf bag, it didn't go the way he wanted, making me feel pleased. He climbed into the golf cart and roared off, nearly hitting a venerable Douglas fir that had been there long before fairways and condos. I still remember the tree's Latin name: *Pseudotsuga menziesii*.

I have, or once did, a knack for memorization. In college I took a class in dendrology and found learning the Latin names for 225 types of plants and shrubs to be relatively easy. Even today, sixty years later, I can identify a tree with its scientific name. Sometimes I utter them out loud like mantras, still reveling in the delightful way they roll off the tongue: *lirodendron tulipifera* or *populus tremuloides.*

I blame dendrology, in part, for my dilemma. Having acquired one of the few A's delivered in that class, my college roommate bet me five dollars I couldn't get a similar grade in what he deemed an impossibly difficult course: Japanese. Beer was involved. I took him up. I won. It changed my life's trajectory.

   Sylvia is right. I have no appetite because of a Japanese sword. It's been buried in closets ever since I came back from Japan in 1948.

  From time to time, I've taken the sword out, oiled it, and contemplated returning it to the rightful owner or their heirs. I know their names. I couldn't forget as much as I tried to do so. Fading minds can recall acts of youth with great accuracy, I hold the sword my hands, feeling a swelling unease. Then the sword goes back in storage. I've used the excuse that after occupying forces left the islands, Japan implemented strict rules governing ownership and importing and exporting of samurai swords. I couldn't just get on a plane, waltz through customs, and take the bullet train to Kyoto packing a 400-year-old sword in my suitcase. That just wasn't legally or culturally possible.

  After being repressed for decades, my angst over the sword has resurrected and demands attention. I keep asking myself: why is this bothering me so? It isn't as if I murdered anyone. I simply stole a sword. The theft created no financial burden; it came from one of the wealthiest families in Japan.

  Apparently, I can no longer justify my actions. I wake up in the wee hours, an anxiety skittering through my body like the current of an electric fence. Its amperage rises and falls but never totally abates. Last night I lay awake for two hours, listening, as much as my ailing hearing would allow, to the tinkling of our neighbor's wind chimes. I'm eighty years old, for God's sake, with life's finishing line in sight. Why bother worrying about anything except the location of my burial plot?

My reluctance to return the sword comes from the memory of a love so potent it makes me tremble. How was I ever capable of such passion?

The mournful voice of Amália Rodrigues, the queen of fado, coming out of the Bose wasn't helping matters any. Listening to this slit-your-wrist genre precedes most investigations of family behavior, especially mine.

Sylvia recently found me standing in the closet holding the cause of my angst. I was trying to gather the courage to unwrap the artifact, hoping that would somehow move me into action. My stomach contracted simply at the thought of looking at the sword. Sylvia wisely left me to fret alone.

She took a sip of wine. "Will you show it to me?"

"The sword? You've already seen it," I said. "Numerous times. There's nothing more to it, really."

"That was years ago. We were still in the Santa Monica house."

I started to argue that looking at it wouldn't do any good when an inner voice told me that excuse had lost its currency. The command had a pretty good kick to it; I've learned the hard way not to ignore its authority.

After dinner we took our wine glasses and went to the bedroom, our rescue mutt Diego traipsing behind. Sylvia sat on the bed and waited. Diego lay down on the floor, watching my every move.

###

In a Japanese home or in a *dojo*, a sword of this stature would be mounted on a rack made specifically for that purpose. I had no intention of making such a display. I knew it must be stored horizontally and, from time to time, the blade should be treated with *choji* oil to prevent rusting. The scabbard was made of a wood called *Nurizaya*, ideal for long-term storage.

I know these things because around 1960, I brought the sword to an appraiser in Los Angeles. I had no intention of selling it. I think I was hoping to find it was of little cultural consequence.

The appraiser was native Japanese, unusual in the sword world. In the US most connected with the sale, appraisal, and use of Japanese swords are former military personnel once stationed in Japan or overeducated oriental *objet d'art* specialists. Some are martial arts devotees of *kenjutsu*, or the art of the sword. When I realized I was dealing with a native son, I almost turned around. I didn't want to be overly scrutinized. I wanted to be affirmed and absolved and therefore gave no hint I spoke or understood Japanese. I held fast to the image of a coarse and direct gaijin. Besides, the appraiser spoke fair if accented English.

My fantasy that the sword had little value faded the moment the appraiser unwrapped it on the counter; he uttered a low, barely audible warbling respectful sigh. Muramasa blades distinguish themselves by the mottled tempering marks on the blade, irregular and looking like dark clouds arriving on a shiny canvas of steel. The blades also have distinct fishbelly shape.

"Definitely not *taba gatana,*" he said to himself, meaning it wasn't common or mass produced.

He also made a soft guttural murmur of approval when, after donning on white cotton gloves, unsheathed the blade. When he looked up from examining the blade, he would not make direct eye contact, his face tight. My stomach began to hurt. This is not what I had planned.

From below the counter, the appraiser produced a cedar box. Inside rested a battered wooden mallet and two brass punches. A serenity came over him, as if performing a Japanese tea ceremony. Using the mallet and punch, he removed the bamboo pins securing the handle to the tang. Then he took off the *tsuba*, or guard, then the *seppa*, collar, and the *habaki* or spacer. All these parts he laid out on the counter in a neat arrangement, each spaced equally apart. I noticed I was holding my breath.

Most Japanese smiths sign their weapons on the area under the handle. Sometimes they chisel a date, too. That was missing but the creator's name was there in five characters. The appraiser examined them, then suddenly drew his head back in surprise and took in a quick intake of breath. He took out a photographer's loupe and looked at the characters again.

He then used the loupe to examine the grain of the sword's steel. His hands shook at little as he held it up to the light.

He set the sword down on the counter.

"May I ask: Where did you get this *katana*?" using the Japanese word for this style of sword. It was an uncharacteristically direct question coming from a Japanese. It took me by surprise.

I stammered through a story that while serving in occupied Japan, an officer friend of mine in charge of a weapon's depot in Tokyo recognized the sword's value and set it aside. He decided he didn't want it and sold it to me for $25.

The story was weak but plausible. For soldiers of the occupation, possession of a Japanese sword was common, even encouraged. In Tokyo, the lowliest GI or enlisted soldier from Australia could go to the imposing Akabane Arsenal and pick out a sword to take home. They were stacked by the thousands, looking like piles of decorative sticks.

The appraiser looked at me curiously and wiped his left eyebrow with the tip of his index finger. It could almost be mistaken for removing a drip of sweat. In Japan, it is a sign of disbelief.

But, with typical Japanese acquiescence, he didn't challenge my story. He merely said: "You are very fortunate. Unless this blade is an outstanding forgery, which it could possibly be, this sword came from the forge of Muramasa Sengo."

I tried to recall if the name meant anything to me. It didn't.

"Muramasa was one of the greatest swordsmiths of the Muromachi period, if not all history. Very rare. I, myself, have never held one before. It is an honor. What are your plans for this sword? If you have none, I would like to purchase it. I would be pleased to give you $2,500 for it."

Surprised, I mumbled something about just needing to have the artifact appraised for estate purposes.

"Very well," he said. "If you change your mind, kindly let me know. It badly needs to be polished. By the way, you should be aware that the swords created by Muramasa Sengo have been known to carry a curse. They say possession brings out the owner's most violent nature."

He gave a brief bow and smiled blithely hoping, I think, that I would want to rid myself of such a burden immediately.

###

I brought the sword out of the closet, laid it on the bed, and unwrapped the dusty and faded black silk *iaito* used to protect the sword during travel. Diego sat like a sphinx in the middle of the bedroom; both he and Sylvia watched me. Like any couple together for decades, Sylvia and I can divine each other's moods and emotions. She now detected a storm within.

Sylvia bent over and touched the blade. It's beautiful," she said, "in a utilitarian way. I'd forgotten how plain it is. Is it worth anything?"

"Apparently so. Over 30 years ago, an appraiser offered me $2,500. It was probably worth a lot more. I have no idea what the value is now."

"Why don't you have a new appraisal?"

I shook my head. "It's not money I'm after."

"Then what is it, Theodore? What do you want to do with this, this *thing*?" I could hear end-of-my-tether exasperation in her voice and thought a muttering of Portuguese obscenities were to follow. But she kept calm. "When I wake up at three in the morning and you're not in bed and find you at the window, staring out into the dark like a zombie, I know something's wrong.

You're losing weight. You're already too thin. Do you need to see a doctor?"

Sylvia puts, as do most Brazilian women with close connections to their native country (her mother was from Lisbon), great stock in honest conversation. But like most of Portuguese lineage, she understands and accepts that every human has a dark, tragic side and that all the conversation in the world isn't going to change that, and it probably shouldn't either. The Portuguese have a word for it: *saudade*, a longing for an experience that once brought pleasure. It's more acute than nostalgia.

Sylvia's Scottish father, however, made her realize that a life of longing keeps us frozen in sentimentality. He believed that if there was a problem, there was a solution. Moreover, the degree in international law she acquired at Edinburgh permanently infused Sylvia with Caledonian pragmatism.

Sylvia changed tact. "You told me once it brings back a bad memory, yes? Painful even," she said, her voice so soft it almost rustled.

From the living room came the refrains of Rodrigues' melancholy crooning about the dark nights of her soul.

I appreciated Sylvia's empathy. She knew the truncated story behind the sword. We both knew that cratered love is as common as pond water. Sorrow haunted Sylvia's romantic life before we married. I nodded, still not wanting to get into the details. Then I felt my anxiety spike. Something was roiling, welling up from deep within, unstoppable. I felt it but mostly in my stomach; as if someone had belted me in the solar plexus. Shallow breathing constricted my chest. I was having a panic attack or a coronary or both, I thought.

Sylvia was looking at me, eyes wide with concern. I managed to take a deep breath. The air rushing into lungs brought relief and a revelation: not only did the sword represent love gone bad, it was something about my brother Peter and how he died at the hands of the Japanese. I felt ambushed, bewildered and – honestly – pissed. I thought I had made peace with Peter's death decades ago or at least buried it somewhere in a permanent grave. What the hell was it doing back in my life? I took another deep breath. I wanted to tell Sylvia but didn't dare give voice to this discovery.

One confession at a time.

Sylvia thought she had overstepped. She put her hand on my arm. "Teddy, are you OK? You're pale. Look, we don't have to talk about any past love. In fact, I'd rather we didn't."

Again, I appreciated her honesty. Calm and rational as Sylvia could be, a caldronous jealousy simmered close to the surface. She never had much patience with me giving attention to other women, although it would be a stretch to call me a flirt.

"If you don't want to sell it," she said, "why not just give it away, like to a museum? I'm sure you'd find takers."

"Oh, I don't know," I sighed, pushing aside my reluctance and acknowledging that Sylvia was trying to help me. "You're right. It needs to be out of my life. Out of our lives."

In silence we looked at each other, knowing we had taken the first step: an agreement the sword needed to be gone. I was in a state of push-pull: relief at moving forward but also apprehensive at this newly plumbed memory of Peter.

Sylvia looked at me with those observant hazel eyes "You know what I think? I think you need to talk to Alice. Why don't we drive down to Tucson this week? I'll go play a round of golf with Edith while you have coffee or something with Alice."

Alice is the sole offspring from my first marriage. She is everything I am not: voluble, profane, candid, unbound, and determined to live her life as she sees fit. Following in my father's footsteps, I married an emotional bomb thrower first time around. Yet the trait of inherited characteristics blessedly left out my first wife's impetuousness. While non-conformist to her core, Alice turned out to be a student of the human condition. She earned a doctorate in clinical psychology and was in private practice for about 15 years before throwing in the towel. She lives alone with two dogs, having sent both her husbands packing.

Her passions are dogs and adolescent children, curious for a woman with no offspring. But it's a much better fit for her than being a therapist. You want an advocate? Go see Alice. She works part-time for two Tucson high schools as a guidance counselor.

Most importantly considering the current situation, Alice knows me better than any soul on earth. And because she's my daughter, she can plumb my insecurities without threatening me. An insoluble thread binds us, singular in that there were years when she lived with her mother and I saw her very little. There's no hazard of an emotional retreat or abandonment.

It is through Alice's gentle conversations that I came to grasp how much the unconscious world rules our realm. That must be what was happening to me now. For the first half of my life, I had no idea what that term – the unconscious – meant, silly, I know for man of my education and reading. I knew you could build a wall around people and events, sealing them away. I was good at that. I wasn't so adept at acknowledging how these powerful uncontrollable currents cannot be caged. I began to see the force of the unconscious when interrogating captured Japanese officers. These educated and worldly men were often automatons, puppets with strings pulled by deeply imprinted dictatorial spirits.

II

Schisms and Connections

I grew up in a town split by nature and mankind. The railroad tracks, veins of commerce, had been laid through the center of Pocatello before the town had a name. But the Portneuf River had run through the valley eons before the epoch of steel, welling up from multiple springs high on the Bannock Range on the Fort Hall Indian reservation.

The works of man conflicted with the works of the divine. The Portneuf overran its banks from time-to-time, sometimes violently, letting Pocatello and the Oregon Short Line know who had primacy. It sent people to high ground on either side of the valley. My father, in his wisdom, had bought a hillside house with a view of the river from our front porch. Elevation gave us safety, even when the river was in its most biblical moods.

These floods bolstered my sense of security. I never worried, even for a boy with an active imagination, that the river would ever reach our steps. Such was the faith I had in my father's judgment. I took pleasure in knowing our little neighborhood was hermetically cut off from the rest of the town. My father did too, although he made a show of missing work.

My father was a horticulturalist for the Idaho state extension service. Bookish, favoring the classics and scientific literature, he loved the beauty and order of taxonomy. He owned one good suit and distained ostentation or any quest for riches. Gentleness ran deep in his bones. I never heard him yell or utter a harsh word except the occasional guttural cry of exasperation, mostly in dealing with my older brother, Peter.

As I grew older, I became aware of a hereditary burden, which, like Pocatello, operated on a schism. My father used the logic of science and the Linnean world as a shield against a chaotic universe. He avoided addressing messy, non-linear, human problems. He felt that grace – the unmerited love of God and a concept essential to Lutheranism – had eluded him, although he still obliquely pursued it. He recognized that his chosen substitute for this divine benevolence – the Greek ideal, the noble stoic wise in deed and action – would never pack the water necessary for salvation. Through these two opposing concepts, he wound through life treading a tortured road with humility and deference as the main guides. It was a fine case of adaptation, I suppose.

I am my father's son. Seven decades later, I still love order and tradition yet admire those who dare to change and rearrange their lives and society around them. The dance between these two feuding ideals riveted me as early as junior high school when I began taking out

Asian history texts from the Carnegie Library. I was intrigued with the idea that in 30 short years Japan went from a backward, feudal, and polarized nation to one that defeated its two powerful neighbors, China and Russia, in battle. With astonishing speed, they took technology and ideals from other nations and forged these imports to fit the Japanese ideal.

No such interest in historical complexities or on the paradoxical nature of one's soul burdened my hotheaded brother. My father deduced the source of Peter's inner tempest to my mother's family. He gave voice to these observations in a detached and oblique way, as if he were describing the inevitably of some Darwinian species differentiation. My mother's family had emigrated from Calabria – the toe of the Italian boot – and had converted to Mormonism. But for some members, the conversion didn't last or it only stuck half way. My mother wandered around in a spiritual mélange of jack-Mormonism and Catholicism. She never surrendered her wine with meals nor her dramatic view of the world.

I know these attributes by stories only. I remember nothing of my mother. She never recovered from my difficult birth; six months later when the influenza of 1919 came to call, she succumbed.

My father, a widower and not yet remarried, would sometimes relieve the housekeeper and cook by taking me in the field. I can still recall the smells: the rich coppery tang of irrigation water as it hit the hot and freshly plowed fields mixed with the scent of sagebrush after a rain, all combined with the whiffs of pipe tobacco. The scents didn't compare, however, to the pleasure of being alone with my father in the front seat of the chain-driven REO truck the extension service had purchased for my father's travels.

During these trips, I observed my father's behavior and learned to navigate the landmines that lay below the surface of 1920s Pocatello. Although the southern part of the state had generally been spared the viciousness of the strike-ridden mining regions of the north, violence interrupted on a regular basis.

Money, or lack of it, was the prime source of discord. No one was particularly shocked when a trapper, hired to rid an irrigation canal of hole-digging muskrats, killed a farmer with a shovel over an argument over who should get what percentage of the rodent's tanned pelt. The record prices for wheat and wool caused by the war came crashing down about a year after they signed the armistice. Grain elevators bulged from lack of customers. Land foreclosure notices became a feature in the local newspaper. Farmers and bankers squared off.

Moreover, Pocatello was as Balkanized as eastern Europe, with divisions being drawn between racial and religious lines. The federal government kept snipping away at the Ft. Hall Indian reservation. By the time I was in high school, the Bannocks and the Shoshone had a quarter of their original holdings left. The tribes blamed the Mormons, who kept agitating for greater access to reservation land. Except for buying supplies, Indians were not welcome in town, which was mostly controlled by the members of the Church of Latter-Day Saints.

Then there were the pockets of immigrants, Irish and Italians mostly, who came with the railroad. They controlled Pocatello's liquor trade in prohibition-era Idaho, an activity not given to niceties and civil behavior. They kept to themselves. Yet because they were white and of European ancestry, their children became part of the community.

The same could not be said for the Japanese. They suffered the fate of being simultaneously disliked – even hated – and admired. I still recall the first time I bore witness to this contradiction. We were heading down the hill from our house one spring morning and, as the truck crossed the river, I inquired as to our destination.

"To the Christensen place," he said. "Do you remember that farm? Just south of town. I've taken you there before."

I remembered the place and didn't like it. "Do they have a mean big dog that barks and shows his teeth?"

"That's the one. Does that dog scare you?"

"Yes."

"I'm not fond of him, either, but we're not going to the house. We'll be out in the fields. Don't have to worry about the dog."

"You going to look at plants?"

"The plants aren't in the ground yet. I'm going to be talking about growing plants."

"What kind of plants?"

"Potatoes."

"Are the potatoes sick?"

"You mean blighted?"

My father demanded proper terms, even from a six-year-old.

"Let's hope not," he said.

"Then why are we going to see Mr. Christensen?"

"I have to meet with Mr. Christensen and a man from the bank."

Made no sense to me. "Why does the man who works at a bank have to talk to Mr. Christensen about potatoes?"

My father, puffed on this pipe, contemplated my query. He spoke to me as an adult, which pleased me. "Well, you remember what banks do?"

"They give people money."

"Wouldn't that be nice?" said my father. "No, they're not quite in the same class as Santa Claus. They actually lend money. It has to be paid back. Mr. Christensen wants to expand his potato production but he doesn't have enough money to buy the seed potatoes. So, he wants to borrow money from the bank to buy the seeds."

"Oh. And he has to pay the money back?"

"Yes, at the end of the season."

"When they dig up the potatoes, you mean?"

"Yes."

"How come you have to be there?"

"It's my job to encourage the banker to loan Mr. Christensen the money. I have an ally, Mr. Takahashi. He will be there, too.

"Oh. How come Mr. Takahashi has to be there?"

"Mr. Takahashi knows more about growing potatoes than any man in Idaho."

I didn't think this was possible. No one knew more about plants than my father. "Even more than you?"

"Yes, indeed. If he says the acreage Mr. Christensen wants to plant will produce lots of potatoes, then the banker will loan the money."

"What if Mr. Takahashi says the field won't grow lots potatoes?"

"Then the bank might not loan Mr. Christensen the money."

"Mr. Christensen wouldn't like that, would he? He would be mad at Mr. Takahashi."

"He likely would, but I don't think that's going to happen. I've already spoken with Mr. Takahashi. He said he would vouch for Mr. Christensen's ability to grow potatoes and the fertility of his land."

"So does Mr. Christensen have to pay Mr. Takahashi when he digs up his potatoes?"

My father laughed and reached over and rubbed my head. "Oh, I'd like to live in your world, Teddy. But I don't think Mr. Christensen has that kind of charity in him. He sees the Japanese as useful as needed, but otherwise to be ignored. The Japanese are the best growers of potatoes and sugar beets in the upper Snake River Valley and that kind of scares people like Mr. Christensen."

I didn't understand this last comment and was about to ask for an explanation when I saw three men standing beside a headgate, watching the approaching car. We slowed down. One man, Mr. Takahashi, was at least a foot shorter than the other two men. He had a shovel in hand. "Apparently we're a tad late," remarked my father in voice tinged with self-criticism. Being late meant you were wasting people's time and my father, forever concerned with burdening others, did not like that.

Mr. Takahashi gave my father a short bow as he approached.

I was to sit in the truck during the negotiations. I worried that somehow Christensen's pony-sized dog would find its way out into the field. But admiring thoughts of my father were paramount. Society profoundly underestimates how astutely children zero in on the heart of adult matters. I had picked on my father's ability to strategize and make things happen without confrontation or conflict. His admiration for the Japanese, whom he saw as marginalized, was not lost on me either.

My father found deep kinship with these immigrants. As Confucians, they appreciated education; in my father they saw a learned man. They also found sympathy in his quiet demeanor and propensity to listen rather than talk. It's been said that the only difference between and a Swede and a Japanese is the jolt in his booze (whisky vs sake) and the color of their hair. The two nationalities dovetailed on their conflict avoidant behavior. I could sense the uplifting of my father's spirits when extension dispatched him to a consultation involving a Japanese farmer.

None gave him more pleasure than visiting the Takeda brothers, Gensai and Kuwahara. For starters, they ran a truck farm and a nursery; their concerns delved into the heart of my father's horticultural pleasures. If he had his way, my father would have spent all day focusing on small fruit production, expounding on ground covering plants and the developments of ornamentals. He didn't have that luxury. Paucity of funds at extension forced him to be a jack-of-all-trades agronomist, offering advice on smuts, lectures on soil amendments, and workshops on sugar beet entomology.

Secondly, Kuwahara was the closest thing my father had to a friend. I have no recollection of Ken – his Americanized name – ever socializing with my father beyond these visits; but I have a distinct memory of watching them sitting on a bench under an ornamental cherry in bloom, drinking coffee, smoking, my father with his pipe and Ken's with his self-rolled cigarettes, talking, utterly in their own world.

Watching the Takeda brothers taught me how families endure under adversity. Ken was the younger of the two brothers. The eldest brother, Gensai, was a taciturn and peevish bachelor, not to mention short and homely. He refused to take an English name and spoke choppy and guttural English and barked at his younger brother and his wife. But my father respected his plant knowledge and financial acumen.

Yet, it was the ying that pulled my father towards the Takedas more than the yang.

My mother had been volatile and argumentative. My father's current cook and housekeeper, my mother's cousin, was only marginally more pacific. Prone to over-indulgence in home-vinted wine, she could be mercurial and moody and sang off-key arias in Italian when working in the kitchen. In Peter, my father had a son who tipped over bee hives, commandeered a neighbor's horses – riding them bareback – and tossed green apples through the stained windows of the Episcopal Church.

While my father stoically shouldered these burdens, blaming himself for our wobbly home life and Peter's actions, he yearned for the calm of the Takeda home. Mrs. Takeda spoke but a smattering of English yet she seemed determined to communicate her welcome and warmth. She doted on my father; I watched him glow with pleasure as she fussed over him.

She also paid attention to me.

The first time I ever went with my father for a visit to the Takeda nursery, he told me I could walk around but I must keep the truck in sight. I passed the time by herding a colony of ants, clearing paths for them as they trooped to and fro their nest. I looked up to find Mrs.

Takeda approaching with a mug and a bowl. Startled, I thought about running back to the safety of the truck.

Holding the mug and bowl, she knelt, gracefully and precise as a bird landing on a branch and gave me the tiniest of bows. She set down the mug and bowl in front of me.

"Sweet tea," she said, then moved her hand above the bowl, "and lice cake." My child's literalist brain immediately imagined a cake made of a thousand lice but, the next instant, saw that the little mounds were made with grains of rice covered with caramelized sugar. Mrs. Takeda gave the smile of a doting aunt, then got up and left.

I instantly developed a crush.

There was another reason I began enjoying these visits: my presence had been discovered by the Takeda's youngest daughter, Sumi. We later discovered our birthdays were within 12 days of each other. She and I experienced similar circumstances. Her two eldest sisters were off at school and she sought a playmate.

I first saw her carrying a tray nearly as big as herself. We spotted each other simultaneously through a row of trees and she stopped, letting the tray hang by her side. Then she neatly placed the tray on the grass and walked over to me. Even as a preschooler, Sumi had learned the Japanese obligation of taking care of guests. She had abandoned, however, any oriental shyness.

"Who are you?" she demanded.

I just stared. While she wore the clothes of an ordinary American five-year-old girl, a plain, faded yellow dress, obviously a hand-me-down, and scuffed brown shoes, her beauty and black eyes rendered me dumbstruck. I had never seen a girl like this. She waited a polite beat.

"My name is Sumi," she said, and then waited again for me to speak.

When again I said nothing she simply took my hand and commanded, "you come."

In a gesture that I would repeat over and over in life with women, I followed.

Sumi was on a mission to collect empty tea cups and whatever crockery her uncle Gensai had carried from the main house to his two-room bungalow. The inner decor fixated me: absolute order, simplicity, and the smell and texture of the tatami mat in Gensai's bedroom. I had to touch the mat to feel its smoothness, even though I knew I shouldn't. I asked my father about the tatami on the way home. He admonished me for going into Gensai's home, even though I had been invited, then explained to me that Gensai was "old school," and preferred to stick to Japanese ways.

While my own home nowhere reached the entropy levels of, say my Italian cousins in Twin Falls, where plate throwing and shouting matches were a regular occurrence, it lacked solidity and calm. As a young child subconsciously seeking security, the Takeda home fulfilled that need. Mrs. Takeda's affection, her beautiful daughters, the order, the contained world, and the ability to adapt and endure, cemented a deep-seated interest in the Japanese. It also sowed within me affection, if not a downright weakness, for Japanese women.

Only through more seasoned eyes did I see that such order comes at a cost. When that sense of stability is threatened, authoritarianism and rigid hierarchy act as assuaging agents. On the surface, everything functions as smoothly as a Swiss watch, but only because there is an obligation to obey and not make waves. This dynamic leads to the illusion of superiority and a spurning of any criticism. A type of heinous blinkeredness sets in. In its own way, Japanese insularity can rival that of the Chinese or the council of Cardinals in Rome.

III
Shame (haji) is the root of all virtues. Tell no one

It wasn't until later in the day when Alice and I got together. Sylvia and Edith couldn't get a tee time until mid-afternoon. They would play a round then Sylvia would join us for dinner. Because we were a late in our arrival into Tucson, Sylvia dropped me off at Alice's driveway, squeezed my hand supportively, pulled my head towards her, kissed me on the cheek, shooed an excited Diego out of the car, then drove off.

Alice's two dogs met me at the door, led by the yapping of a one-eyed, half-beagle, half-Chihuahua named Jack. Despite his size, he's definitely the alpha. Limited vision doesn't prevent him from sizing up any visitor, two legged or four. Every soul coming through that door warrants inspection. Then there's the sleek and loving Penny, whose tail constantly wags in a state of contentment. She's a lab-greyhound mix, sleek as an otter, and can slip off a couch with liquid grace of a boa. Both are rescue mutts like Diego and, from their first meeting, accepted him into the brotherhood of dogs granted a second life.

Alice, gray-streaked brunette hair pulled back in a rough ponytail, reading glasses hanging around her neck, was dressed in a tie-dye tank top, blue jean cut offs and flip-flops. She welcomed us, giving me and Diego big hugs. She then ushered the dogs out the back door, advising them it might be a good time to take a dip in her kidney-shaped pool.

Her living room was an ideal temperature, made so by her preference in using an evaporative cooler as opposed to an air conditioner. Alice had a fine collection of Mesoamerican art, pottery, mostly, and a couple of simple Navajo rugs, the really valuable kind. Her bookshelves were stuffed; I recognized a few volumes I'd given her.

When she returned, Alice announced that iced tea or coffee had little appeal. Could I be coaxed into drinking a gin and tonic? One wearies of wine and always waiting for 5:00. She also knew I'd open up easier with a little booze under my belt. Besides, the anxiety that arrived the other night as Sylvia and I looked at the sword had not gone away. Its strength frightened me and I could feel it yearning for recognition and oxygen. A drink wouldn't hurt.

She set the glasses down on the coffee table and plopped herself in a worn armchair. Alice didn't beat around the bush. "Dad, you like look Eeyore with a hangover. What's going on?"

"That obvious, eh? Old ghosts are paying a call, I guess."

"The audacity of them. What kind of ghosts?"

I didn't know what to say, so I just said: "The kind that won't go away."

Alice nodded her head in approval at my honesty. "Any idea where they're from?"

"Couple places, I think. Probably the biggest one of them stems from romance gone bad and me acting badly."

"Don't tell me you're have an affair," she said, laughing, looking over the top of her glass.

"No. No. God no."

She waited. Humor might loosen the old man up.

"Old romance," I said, in the way of an explanation.

"How old?"

I took a deep breath then a sip of my drink. Then I took a proper gulp, listening to the hum of the evaporative cooler. "Happened when I was stationed in occupied Japan. This romance," I stopped. "Hell, listen to me. It wasn't a romance. That's a sanitized word for the torrid, passionate affair that it was."

"Wow. You've never told me about this. This is juicy."

This made me a little prickly. "Last I knew, fathers aren't in the habit of indulging their daughters with tales of their pre-marital sex life. Besides, it was one of those events that once buried, best lies undisturbed. That's the rationale, anyway. Don't tell anyone. Don't give it oxygen. It may smolder but it won't catch fire."

"But it's burning now?"

"A full-on conflagration. Haven't slept worth a damn for a month."

"That's not so good. You want to tell me about it?"

"Well, in a nutshell. I fell madly in love and got dumped."

She gave a sigh of empathy. "Ouch. But it's a 50-year-old ouch, yes?

"Fifty years exactly. She cut off the relationship on May 5th, 1946. Boys day, or *Tango no Sekku,* as they'd say in Japan.

"Who was "she?" asked Alice.

"Noriko Shibusawa," I said. When I spoke her name, it felt as if I just chugged a gallon of ice water.

Alice put her glass down and waited, her joking attitude gone. When I said nothing for about 30 seconds, Alice said. "When you mentioned her name, it looked like someone slugged you."

"I have not said her full name – not out loud – for half a century."

"Wow," she said again, but this time the word carried real concern and gravitas.

I nodded in agreement. Alice waited.

"We were going to get married. Live in the Bay Area or someplace in southern California. Have kids. The full catastrophe, to quote Zorba."

Then the words stopped. A muffler-less motorcycle roared by on the street.

"And?" said Alice finally

"I'm not sure I can explain it at the moment. What I need help with is resolving what happened after the breakup. I tried, of course, to get Noriko to change her mind. I wanted reconciliation so badly. I never wanted anything so badly in my life."

I felt my throat start to thicken; I wanted to obey the lifelong habit of swallowing my sorrow. I pushed forward, however. "But for her, there was no going back. It was over. I went into a tailspin. Started hitting the sauce pretty hard. One night after drinking myself into a stupor at a sake bar, I went to her apartment and hammered on the door. No one answered and I was sure she and her maid were in there."

"Her maid?"

"Yes. Her maid. Noriko came from quite a storied family. Anyway, no one answered so I just busted the door down."

"You? Busted down a door?"

"Yes, me. Well, I didn't actually bust it down. It was a sliding door and pretty flimsy. I just forced the lock. I still remember the door flying sideways. Turns out Noriko wasn't home after all. Neither was her maid. Noriko probably anticipated confrontation and, in typical Japanese fashion, took action to avoid it. God, Alice, I wish the story ended right there. But I was enraged. I had been denied. I was sure I could convince her to come back to me."

Alice shook her head and sighed. "Oh, Dad. And you've kept this in all these years?"

"Sylvia said the other day that everyone's had love affairs gone bad. We've all got to deal with it and move on. Like I said, I've reasoned that the best way to keep those memories from haunting me too badly is to stick them in the emotional deep freeze. Anyway, standing in Noriko's bedroom in the dark, shaking with anger, I remembered that she had something that she treasured. Actually, she didn't treasure it so much as her parents and family did and they'd given it to her for safekeeping. It was a sword."

Alice looked at me quizzically. "A sword? Like a samurai sword?"

I nodded and held out my arms as wide as I could. "Yes. A long-bladed samurai sword. A *katana.* It was ancient – hundreds of years old – and had been in the family for generations. Ordinarily, it would have been kept in one of the family's grand houses. Apparently, they had many. But at the start of the occupation, GI's were ordered to go from house to house and collect all weapons, including swords. There were not supposed to be any actually searches of homes; but the Shibusawa family had ties to the militarist faction in Japan. Their factories had made some particularly vile munitions and some of the Army brass was inclined to make the family really feel the sting of occupation. Noriko's family thought by hiding the sword in her humble apartment, of which the occupants were two single women, it would be safe."

I paused. "But they weren't counting on someone like me."

"Then what happened?"

"I knew where the sword was: Noriko had made the mistake of showing me once: behind the false wall in the back of a closet. I didn't even need to turn on any lights. I went to the closet and slid open the door. I could smell her. That pushed my anger to new heights. I seized the bedding and clothes her maid had so carefully stored in there, all stacked neat as a neurosurgeon's refrigerator. I threw them out on the tatami. I remembered watching Noriko work her fingers through a gap in the top of the wall and pulling it down. I did the same and down the wall came, at least enough for me to see the dark, long lump mounted on the real wall. The sword was wrapped in silk, so it didn't look like a sword at all, just a vague shape. But I knew what it was. I took it. I went back to my room at the hotel and passed out on my bed, still fully clothed. When I awoke, I didn't remember anything, not at first anyway. But I recall being overwhelmed with the haunting feeling. Then I got up and discovered the sword."

Even though I'd been sipping this G&T, a dryness borne of anxiety persisted in the back of my throat. I sat back in my chair and took a long drink, letting the lime and quinine bitters ease my condition. Are you going to clam up as usual, I asked myself, then wait for the kick-in-the-ass of outside forces to say what you need to say?

"So, Alice. I did what most people – besides you – in our family did. I pretended it didn't happen. I kept waiting for the police or Noriko or someone from her family to show up at my door or some security detail from Dai-ichi – that was MacArthur's headquarters in Tokyo where I worked – to darken my door. But no one came. The more time passed, the deeper I buried the incident."

"And you never went back to Noriko's apartment?"

I shook my head. "Never saw her again."

"Not even when you went back to Japan on business."

"Not even then. Not even when I was in Kyoto which is where she lived."

"But you thought about it?"

"Oh yes, indeed. Constantly," I said. "But I disciplined myself to stay away."

"What about this event bothers you so? What gives it such staying power, Dad?" she asked.

"Noriko didn't deserve any of this. I can't imagine the shame she had to bear for losing that sword. I had it appraised once. It's extremely rare and valuable but that's not the point. For a Japanese to disappoint your inner circle, your family, your clan, with such laxity is very serious and damaging. I sometimes wonder why she didn't commit suicide."

"How do you know she didn't?"

"Because I followed her life since then, although not so much the last ten years."

Alice raised her eyebrows disapprovingly but said nothing. She never liked the way my job gave access to the details of people's lives.

"Sure. I mean, Alice. Our firm could find information on just about anybody in the world. Noriko, with her family background, wasn't that hard to track. She married and had three children."

"Are you still in love with her?"

I inwardly groaned, my reaction to Alice's unstinting ability to hit the central nerve. Retreat! But no, I had to do this. Still, I did take a big swallow, practically draining my glass.

"The fire of a big love never disappears," I said. "It just dies down enough so you can stand the heat. The years pass. You don't obsess about it and life goes on. But Noriko still appears in my dreams. What can I say?"

"Dad. How about not worrying about what to say but rather try to plumb the core issue, the central emotion inside? Can you put your finger on that? What is it about this incident that has such resilience and keeps you up at night half a century? Don't think too hard. You're not going to offend me."

"Well, Alice," I stopped, not wanting to say the words but my emotions were not to be denied. "I think the act of dishonor plays a central role here."

"Dishonor? Dishonor for whom?" she asked.

"Dishonor for both us, but mostly for me. I keep asking myself: why, of all people, did I think I could get away with this? No one totally knows a people, a national pathos, of course, but I flattered myself that I understood the Japanese psyche."

"And you feel, what? Guilty about using this knowledge?"

I looked up, words flowing involuntarily, despite the fact they burned me like fire as they exited. "No, Alice. It's not guilt. No. It's shame that I wanted to inflict shame on others. I had traded on my intimate knowledge of the Japanese. Shame. That's what, year after year, ate away at me. The act was so calculating. I wanted to hurt Noriko, make her pay. I knew the wound the disappearance of the sword would create. It would isolate Noriko from her family. She would forever live with a sense of shame and dishonor."

Alice said nothing.

"Shame was one of the primary tools in my interrogator's arsenal. I was good because I was neither a bully nor a breaker, as they are called in the trade. Instead, I learned to employ the three s's with my Japanese prisoners: sympathy, statistics, and shame. First and foremost, I learned that in being captured, these men had violated the concept what the Japanese call *ko on*, or loyalty or obligation to the emperor and to Japan. I saw what capture did to them. It broke them. Dishonored them. Their life as Japanese had ended. I wanted to inflict that same sense of hurt on Noriko."

I expected Alice to say something truthful and blunt, which would have been her style, something like, 'wow, that's pretty vindictive.' Instead she said:

"So, Dad, help me understand. It's a sense of opportunism, maybe? That constituted a lack of honorable action? That you manipulated someone, hurt them, in order to assuage your own hurt? That's the shame?"

I nodded, unable to speak, her distillation going through me like spears. My eyes filled but strangely I felt no embarrassment for shedding tears in front of my adult daughter. I had never wept in Alice's presence before nor any of my children.

Alice fetched a box of tissues from the side table and set it down in my lap. Then she sat beside me, reached up and wrapped her arms around my shoulders and leaned on me. We sat there, silent but for the tears, tears that contained the energy of ancient act. They kept splashing down the front of my shirt, the product of small sobs that wouldn't cease. From the backyard, we heard a series of splashes then a volley of barking. It was such a joyous sound, dogs having fun in the water on a warm October day.

"Can they get out of the water OK?" I asked, blowing my nose, relieved to be occupied with a vision of Diego struggling to find his way out of the pool.

"They always do. But do you want to see for yourself?"

We walked to the back door. More barking. I could identify one of the voices as Diego's. There he was at the pool's edge, soaking wet, barking as Jack and Penny chased a tennis ball around in the pool. Diego had been in and somehow gotten himself out. Of course he had.

As we stood at the door, I spoke, again almost involuntarily, not sure of the source of my words but not worrying about filtering them out, either.

"That life Noriko and I had planned had such solidity, such certainty."

I shook my head, wondering about my youthful naiveté. "You know what I've figured out? We live lives but usually that "life" isn't enduring. Life is about chapters. But it's hard for us to imagine that there will be a next chapter. We get deluded into permanence. That's what being 80 has taught me. Epochs open and close unexpectedly. Look at me: a dreamy, brainy stork of a kid from Pocatello who – due to the whims of war – got pulled into intelligence services, ended up in Hawaii first as an interpreter then, of all improbabilities, an interrogator. Then it was onto Japan in '46 and me thinking: so, this is what I do. I'm going to spend the rest of my life as a Japanese specialist. There was this finality."

Alice turned and looked right at me. She took both my hands and looked at me.

"But that finality wasn't there, was it? The hardest memories to forget stem from people with whom we have unresolved issues."

Alice's words so resonated I didn't know what to say at first. Alice gently kneaded my knuckles of my right hand. Finally, I said, "Ironically, my relationship with Noriko couldn't have seemed more permanent. We would marry and move back to the US. Then just as suddenly the chapter closed. My relationship with the Army came to an end. I could have stayed in Japan but I knew it was time to go. Wanted to put the country behind me. Within two years, I ended up marrying your mother, a woman as different from Noriko as one can imagine. I thought that this, finally, was going to be a permanent station or situation. Yet that ended like just any other chapter."

Alice released my hands. "How are you feeling? Want another drink?"

I waved her off. "I better not. Sylvia will get mad if she comes back and finds me drunk as a skunk."

"Dad, for God's sake. Stop acting like Atticus Finch. As ghosts go, you've just described is a whopper. Give yourself permission to get blotto, if necessary. Stop worrying about Sylvia and besides, I think she'd understand. What does she know about this?"

"Edited version only. I got jilted and I stole a sword. That's it. She knows I don't like to talk about it."

"What the worst that can happen if you give her the full story?"

"She may be seventy but that Latin blood of hers gets stirred up over stuff like this and when it does, it's no picnic at 1914 East Mesa Court. No need to chuck rocks at a hornet's nest."

"That just means she's still crazy about you," she said. "I would encourage you that the moment you feel it's all right to tell Sylvia more, go ahead and take that risk.

Maybe this will never happen. And that's OK if it doesn't."

I nodded. "You're right. Of course you're right. Sure, pour me another. A short one, though. It doesn't take much to get me gassed these days."

We walked back to the living room with our drinks and sat back down.

Alice asked. "You sure you want to talk about this other ghost? Or is that too much? Maybe we want to talk about something else, something mundane as goddamn Arizona politics?"

I shook my head, although I actually would have welcomed a change in conversation, so adverse was I to bringing up the next topic. But I knew I must forge on. The tears and gin had loosened me up. I did not want to die trapped by the anger concerning my brother's death.

"All right," she said.

"This ghost. It's about Peter," I said, barely audible, a croak, really.

Alice knew that Peter had died at the hands of Japanese interrogators, which was true enough but not the whole story. She sat back in her chair and covered her mouth but said nothing.

"I've never spoken to anyone about this, not in any detail. I figured you'd be proud of me. I've deduced this much: The ghost isn't Peter per se any more than Noriko's ghost is all about her. It's about my interaction with parts of their lives, my role. Last week I stood in my closet holding that damned sword. I was trying to get up the courage to unwrap it, thinking maybe that help me get off my ass but I just couldn't. Something was stopping me. Then, a few days ago, Sylvia wanted to see the sword. My instinct said no, but something in me made me do it anyway. In the process, I realized the paralysis wasn't only stemming from my dishonorable act with Noriko but from the fact that the sword reminded me of what happened to Peter. I think I'm still desperately angry at what the Japanese did to him."

I paused, did an involuntary swallow, and took a sip. It was mostly tonic water, which was probably a good thing. I shook my head. "Alice, it seems that the gods decided early on in life to grant me access to privileged knowledge. My position in Japan gave me access to information about Peter's death. The timing, well, the timing was nothing short of serendipitous. When I was involved with Noriko, I sought a classified document about what happened to him. And one morning, it arrived on my desk."

"I see," said, Alice, taking a deep breath and pushing her head back even further in the chair as if shoved by the force of my words. "And what did you find out?"

"You don't want to know." I said.

"You're right. I don't. But it was horrible, no doubt."

"I will just say that it involved vivisection."

Alice held out her hand. "Stop, Dad. I mean it. I know you need to talk about this but I'm not the right person to hear the details about how my uncle died, as much as I wish I were. I'm a real wuss when it comes to stuff like this."

Ordinarily I would have shut up but something in me wasn't taking no for an answer. "Please Alice, bear with me. What happened, happened. I can't change that. It doesn't help that all the perpetrators involved in Peter's death got their sentences commuted and eventually walked out of prison. They were supposed to end up in the hangman's noose. But if they all dangled their way into eternity, I wouldn't feel any differently. My anger goes beyond revenge. I'm not sure I understand that. As I said, I'm pretty familiar with the workings of the Japanese psyche. Many of the men, the ones who ran POW camps, the ones responsible for heartless and inhumane and unthinkable treatment of prisoners, had been raised, since childhood, to see themselves as superior. People of a divine race, better than all. Even members of their own who had fallen were less than human. You should have seen the distain at which the Japanese treated their wounded, as if getting shot or loaded with shrapnel and surviving was some sort of crime. Jesus! Their own men! Defies belief. All the punishment in the world wouldn't get them to understand what they did was ghastly. And perhaps death was the fitting consequence for their action. I'm not smart enough to figure that out. Somehow, I've got to come to some reconciliation."

I suddenly felt bombarded and knocked around, like Mohammad Ali had clocked me from the right, then Joe Frazier had hammered one in from the left. But there was also an accompanying feeling of deflation and release. I tried to ignore it, chalking it up to the gin, but something about the inner conflict was different.

Alice eyes on me, soft as velvet, asked me how I was doing.

"OK, I guess. As we're having this conversation, I can honestly tell you that the rage isn't as strong as it was even three days ago. Is that possible? But you can imagine how I felt when I was 26 years old, reading this classified document, which was written in excruciating detail and simultaneously in love, crazy in love, with Noriko."

"You felt as if you being pulled apart."

"Completely," I said, "and when she left me, everything didn't collapse. It exploded. My rage could no longer be contained. I had to do something for revenge or retribution. Stealing the sword was a manifestation of that emotion, chickenshit as it was."

"It wasn't chickenshit. It was completely understandable," said Alice. "When, in the timeline of your relationship with Noriko, did you find out about your brother's death?"

"Oh, I guess about three months before she left me."

"Dad. You're describing an almost unbearable conflict: the discovery of the gruesome death of your brother at a time when you're being rejected by the love of your life, who also happens to be Japanese."

I hadn't thought about the situation in those terms.

She leaned forward in her chair. "Have a sip of that drink of yours before all the ice cubes melt. You all right? You got anything else in there that needs to come out?"

I shook my head. Then a thought came.

"I keep thinking that I need to heed another lesson I learned from my prisoners."

"What's that?"

"More than a few of these men realized that what happened was beyond their control and that they now found themselves in a situation with a different set of rules. They could either sink or swim. Their sense of that they called *ko on*, or obligation, switched from Japan and the emperor, to embracing reality. They stopped trying to starve themselves or find a piece of hemp to wrap around their neck as punishment. They took responsibility for their lives. Now, maybe, I need to do that, too."

For the first time in weeks, I slept soundly, despite that fact that the mattress on Alice's guest room bed was too hard. The gin and Alice's good cooking probably didn't hurt. I actually had an appetite. I had a wild montage of dreams: watching Peter playing football in Pocatello except all the people in the stands were old, like me. Also having sex with Noriko, me on my back, her riding me aflame with desire and me looking out the window of the bedroom and seeing the landscape of not Tokyo, but Santa Monica. Finally, a brief snippet of me opening the dishwasher after it had run a rigorous pots and pans cycle and yet the dishes inside remained caked in moldy and old food particles. So confusing but not without meaning.

I woke up the next morning and thought – as I do many days: I'm still here. How much longer will I last?

On the drive back to Flagstaff, we took the long way home, avoiding downtown Phoenix. Instead, we opted to take the two-lane roads through the rim country of the Tonto National Forest. I enjoy the drive because the mountains remind me of ranges in southern Idaho. There are few grand, jagged snow-covered peaks, just the pleasure of common rust-colored stratigraphy, majestic in its own way, and swathes of coniferous forest. Some of the drainages, dotted with cottonwoods, can exhibit spectacular foliage this time of year.

Sometimes we stop and go on a small hike. I like to put enough distance between us and the road so all I can hear is silence – besides the constant hissing in my ears – and the wind.

Sylvia likes this route because a few years back, we discovered a restaurant in Payson, ostensibly a touristy Italian grill, with a Portuguese owner who makes a divine caldo verde, a soup made up of onions, potatoes, and kale. It's served with slab of smoked pork sausage and a hunk of rosemary focaccia. I can't decide what I enjoy more: watching Sylvia become delirious with pleasure as she feasts on the food of her childhood or listening to the flowing Portuguese as she gets wrapped up in conversation with Ana Sophia, the owner, two sets of hands flying about and much mirth. They always hug and tear up when they part.

After lunch, we drove about half an hour and, as is our habit on this trip, pulled over near the town of Pine, parking the Camry at a rest stop. There, we eased back our seats and nap. Sylvia woke first and began driving. I groggily awoke only after she stopped to get a coffee. Sips from her cup helped me gain re-entry.

"How did your conversation go with Alice?" she asked.

I had been waiting for this. I didn't fill in all the details such as me keeping track of Noriko for 50 years, but, heeding Alice's advice, I gave Sylvia the fullest version I'd ever allowed to escape my lips. Sylvia wanted a name and I gave it to her.

She seemed unfazed but I noticed her tapping her fingers on the steering wheel in irritation, looking out the driver's side window a few times, listening, nodding her head, lost in thought, taking stock of her feelings and emotions. Would fiery Mediterranean passion or Scot pragmatism emerge? Often times it's a little of both but at this point I didn't really care. I was plodding forward and she had to appreciate that. But I couldn't bring myself to talk about Peter although I knew, sooner or later, that Sylvia needed to be let in on my revelation.

"But you're feeling better, yes?"

"I think so, yes."

"I noticed you slept through the night and actually ate something. That's an improvement." She paused then turned to me. "I did something you might not like," she said, in a confessional tone.

This made sense. I thought she had exited the conversation about my visit with Alice a little too quickly.

"What?"

"I called Nicholas a few days ago and told him about your dilemma."

"Dilemma?"

"About the sword."

"Oh Sylvia. Why? I wish you hadn't done that. Why can't you let me settle this business on my own?"

We have two sons, Nicholas and Adrian. Adrian, the youngest, is a physicist, and lives in Flagstaff with his wife, Melanie, and two children. They're one of the reasons we moved to Flagstaff. Adrian is the director of the Mount Lowell Observatory. He's low-key, smart, as in love with astronomy as I was with the Japanese culture and his grandfather was with plants. Like me, he's an introvert but also bureaucratically savvy. He's generally at ease with the world and doesn't fret much.

Nicholas, on the other hand, works for the State Department, and is patently ambitious. Fluent in Portuguese, he's often posted to countries where that's the lingua franca: Portugal, Brazil or Angola, for example. He recently got posted to the Republic of Sao Tome and Principe, a tiny island nation off the Gulf of Guinea. I thought this must be some backwater assignment but he acquired the position of deputy chief of mission, a critical appointment if one wishes to someday become ambassador, which the striving Nicholas indeed does.

"Well, you've just told me that you had a tell-all session with Alice."

My temples began to throb. "Yes, but dear God, Sylvia, that's Alice. She knows when to ask questions and when to leave matters be. Knowing Nicholas, he'll treat the situation like a formal state department inquiry and take over."

"I know *meu amor*," she purred in Portuguese. "I kept the details slim. I mentioned it in passing, casually, like it was a matter of little importance."

"What did you say, exactly?"

"Oh, I said you were cleaning out a closet and found this old Japanese sword and that you thought it was somewhat valuable and maybe you should return it to Japan. But then you recalled that it was quite difficult to bring a sword back to Japan. I then wondered out loud if that was true. That's it."

"And?"

"He said he'd look into it and that was that."

I didn't say anything. Sylvia was right. Handled adroitly, Nick could be an asset in this situation. If we could limit his participation to discovering the legal niceties of returning a sword to Japan, that could be helpful. But then this was Sylvia's way of saying she thought the sword should not only be out of our lives, it needed to be far, far, away. I didn't like being pushed. She wanted this lingering ghost out of our life.

IV

Yamato

I came to Japan seeking the world I'd discovered in books. As a student, I spent days in the University of Michigan library, mooning over woodcuts and ancient Japanese manuscripts. I was on a first-name basis with the overseers of the Oriental special collection, living in the shadow of Hokusai's 36 views of Mt. Fuji and his fifty-three Stations of the Tokaido. I tasted the salt from his famous wave; I huddled down with the 47 ronin as they plotted on how to avenge the death of their noble lord Asano; I reveled in Genji's string of romances and the poetry used in everyday conversation.

My utilitarian soul thrilled when I read the words of Lafcadio Hearn, the Greek-Irishman who knew more about the Japanese psyche than any occidental alive. "We must have meat and bread and butter; glass windows and fire; hats, white shirts, and woolen underwear; boot and shoes; trunks, bags, and boxes; bedsteads, mattresses, sheets, and blankets: all of which a Japanese can do without and is really better off without."

Life in the Army chipped away, day after day, at this idyll. The existence of my projected Japan became so tenuous while working as an interrogator at Camp

Iroquois in Hawaii that I shelved it entirely, comforting myself that world would be waiting for me when the war was over. I kept my vision alive in spite of being confronted by prisoner confessions that described an ideological purgatory of obligation combined with the illusion of superiority.

I maintained my woodcut Yamato even as our bombs flattened and firebombed Japanese cities. The flames burned with such intensity that glass liquefied and canals boiled.

I even preserved my projected world after Peter was killed in 1945.

Peter's funeral alone should have vanquished my dreams. People packed the Pocatello Grace Lutheran church to the rafters. The lieutenant governor showed up. But there were no Japanese in that room, even members of the church's congregation. They didn't dare.

Try going to a military funeral that has no body. An empty coffin has more weight than one filled with a giant. Try walking out of a church, casket upon your shoulders, the whole congregation wondering where Peter's body really was, trying to cement Christian forgiveness over the rage so palpable in the room. The men especially. Some could not understand why I remained in Japan, even though they knew I was a commissioned officer with obligations. I was aiding the enemy who had tortured and killed my brother. "We should have turned that whole place into a glowing mass of embers," said Peter's former high school football coach. "We never should have stopped at Nagasaki and Hiroshima."

I should have despised Japan by then. But no. I chased the country in spite of it all.

I worked for the Tokyo-based Supreme Commander for Allied Powers, which the military, with their penchant for acronyms, invariably referred to as SCAP. I'd been promoted to captain and was an aide-de-camp for MacArthur's assistant chief-of-staff, an unusually loose arrangement. MacArthur demanded loyalty and devotion. But I was just far away from his inner circle to ascertain a degree of independence.

During the war, my comprehension of written Japanese had gone from good to very good. In fact, the Army determined I had a native proficiency in reading and oral comprehension, a professional proficiency in speaking and a working proficiency in writing. There weren't many like me around. My telephone never stopped ringing as I shuttled between the economic, diplomatic, legal, and public information sections of SCAP.

My commanding officer offered solace: he permitted me to arrive as late as 8:30, as interpreting and translating obligations for military or diplomatic functions often took up my evenings. He also gave me Sundays off and, if possible and work permitted, half day on Saturday.

Exciting? Oh, hell yes. But also exhausting. Sometimes I wouldn't collapse into my bed until after midnight. As I had done most of my life, I found at outlet in exercise, morning runs that gave not only relief from overwork but offered me gut level appreciation for Japan's suffering. I would pass block after block of shattered buildings, running past one heap of rubble and ash to another, some areas leveled as flat as a cornfield. Churchill once said the US bombed Tokyo so much the rubble bounced.

The people themselves bore the greatest witness to misery. Not only were there residents trying to rebuild using every imaginable scrap of material but wandering ghosts, the soldiers and farmers and merchants from the former colonies or Manchuria or Taiwan searching for their lost homes. The corpses were gone but the sick and the malnourished were everywhere.

When overwhelmed at work, the East Garden of the Imperial Palace, which had been spared the bombing, provided the easiest refuge. It sat right across the Hibiza moat from the Dai-Ichi building. One morning, I found myself there, lost in thought, staring at massive hand-cut stone blocks that made up the foundation of a former Edo era castle, imagining the effort and human misery it took to get them where they are.

It was late August. Tokyo sat smothered in a tank of humidity. A brisk walk around the block meant a soaked shirt. I learned to move slowly, difficult for a man perpetually short of time.

The male cicadas blasted away their high-pitched whistling love song, singing a sound the Japanese described as, "tsuku-tsuku boshi." A magnificent Japanese elm provided protection from the deceptively hot gauzy sun; but I wearied of being pelted by expired cicadas falling from the branches. A Japanese staffer at Dai Ichi told me that the best thing about cicadas is that they were a harbinger of fall. I had noticed that the previous few nights had carried just a hint of coolness, although I still kept my hotel room ceiling fan over my bed on maximum rotation.

Clouds appeared, providing a temporary shield from the sun. I moved out from the under the tree, my leather soles crunching exoskeletons, the more decomposed ones releasing a sour odor reminiscent of Limburger cheese. Above the insect din, I'd noticed a slightly raspy, insistent bird call. I shaded my eyes and found the creature perched on the branch of a Japanese pine so ancient the gardeners had propped it up with wooden supports. By the pattern of its chest, an elegantly striped vest, I felt mild thrill as I recognized the bird from a Hokusai print titled *The Cuckoo and the Rainbow*.

Behind me came a woman's voice, spoken in beautiful Japanese, almost *kobun* or classical, in nature.

"Since it was of a species unknown in the capital, none of them could identify it."

At first, I thought the voice must be addressing someone else. Yet I knew the line from one of the classics of Japanese literature: *Ise monogatari*, or the *Tales of Ise*. There was no one else around, however. Still, I kept my eyes on the bird, listening. But when the same voice said, in Oxford English, "yes, I am speaking to you, *gaijin*," curiosity forced me to see the source of the erudition and audacity.

She was sitting alone. I guessed her not over 25 years old. There was nothing unusual in her attire, which was thoroughly western: plaid mid-calf skirt, simple hair, unexceptional blouse, and beige cotton jacket, rolled at the sleeves, white ankle socks and polished brown leather flats with a buckle. She was smoking – not common for educated Japanese women, especially in public, particularly in the Imperial Garden – and was by herself, unusual in that the Japanese always go out in groups.

One uncommon feature did stand out, however: she had freckles, a pigmentation seen as a beauty flaw in Japan. Never mind that underneath this milky way of faint red dots lay pale skin and a petite slim face, both considered attractive attributes in Japanese women. I certainly felt a pull.

She moved over on the bench slightly and patted the space beside her. "Please, won't you come join me, if only for a moment?"

For the briefest of moments, I thought I was being solicited, which in a way I was. SCAP had been warned that the Japanese government had hired women, especially those with a high degree of fluency of English, to bed highly placed members of the occupied forces. The government wanted to figure what was really going on in the heads of the inscrutable occidental. Somehow that sounded overly conspiratorial and not necessarily a deterrent to romance.

Moreover, a recent encounter left me rattled. I was out for my morning jog and going through another leveled neighborhood. I had done this route before and the residents were accustomed to seeing this gangly gaijin sweating through their streets. Most gave a crazy, puzzled smile as I passed. Some waved.

That morning, however, I came around a corner and observed a young woman in a knee-length blue dress crossing the street. She stopped briefly, looked at me, then disappeared between two delivery trucks. I thought nothing of it until I reached the two trucks and I heard an urgent voice calling, *gaijin, gaijin.*

I stopped running and turned. She stood between the two vehicles, beckoning with a wave, Japanese style: arm straight out in front, palm down, only her fingers moving slightly back and forth. She was in her late teens and thin, cheeks hollow. I cautiously went toward her, wondering her purpose but suspecting she wanted money. Yet as I approached her, she reached down and lifted her dress to her navel. She had nothing on underneath, revealing a nearly skeletal nakedness, hip bones protruded. She said, in English, "you want me? Two American dollars."

She reminded me of a wild bird, starved to the point of flightlessness, that knows it must risk all for food. I can't remember what disturbed me the most: the fact that this girl, this child, really, was so destitute that she brazenly solicited me in daylight or that I had nothing to give her. I felt such acute embarrassment in my own inadequacy, my own helplessness.

I tried to give her an empathetic smile, knowing I failed, and told her "no thank you," in English. She wasn't giving up. She hiked the dressed up past her tiny breasts. "Please," she said. "One dollar."

I turned my head. Her desperation sliced through the rationalizations I gave for the wretched acts of firebombed cities and horrible misery of those living in Nagasaki and Hiroshima.

My God, I almost wailed out loud, *what the hell am I doing here?*

Moreover, she resorted to this degradation because other American GIs had taken her up on her offer. I turned my pockets inside out; I had nothing in my pocket except my keys. She lowered her dress and disappeared.

I returned numerous times to that street to look for that girl, yen bulging in my pocket, but to no avail.

This woman in front of me, however, carried the air of confidence and intrigue. She wanted something all right but damned if I could figure out what it was. I joined her on the bench. She smiled in satisfaction and offered me a cigarette: Lucky Strikes, the favored smoke of street tarts. I declined.

"Have we met previously?" I asked her in Japanese.

"Not formally, no," she replied in English. "But I have seen you many times. You just haven't noticed me."

"I see," I said, switching to English. "And where did these unequal forms of attention take place?"

"In the Radio Tokyo building. I work for NHK. I just saw you there yesterday."

NHK were the initials for *Nippon Hōsō Kyōkai* or the Japanese Broadcasting Corporation. I had been there yesterday. The radio station had been free with its criticisms of occupying forces, particularly the boorish behavior of our more dimwitted GIs. I applauded the broadcasts. MacArthur and his staff did not. The order had come down from on high to create a code of permissible new stories. Although it was mild censorship by Japanese standards – the press had been forced to be militarist mouthpieces for nearly 30 years – it was censorship none-the-less and I found the task of enforcing it unpleasant.

"Are you a broadcaster?" I asked. "With your exceptional grasp of English I'm sure NHK must have a special place for you."

She gave a high squeaky, crackly laugh, not exactly the ideal radio voice.

"No, no," said she. "The high muck-a-mucks would never dare put me in front of a microphone. I would offend someone within the first minutes. I'm just an editor."

"Where did you learn your English, by the way?"

"At home and in England," she paused and took a delicate puff. She had very good teeth. "My father spent his twenties in London. He spoke to me in English from the time I was born. He returned to Japan and married but went back to England with his family as an attaché with the foreign ministry. I spent five years shivering in the dank halls and rooms of Wycombe Abbey in Buckinghamshire. Have you ever been to Britain?" she asked, with the enthusiasm of a teenager just back from London.

"I went to British Columbia once. Does that count?"

She cocked her head, shot a stream of smoke from the corner of her mouth and gave a wry grin at my cornpone humor. "By the way, I already know your name but I have a high degree of suspicion you do not know mine. I'm Noriko Shibusawa."

We shook hands and simultaneously nodded our heads. The Shibusawa name began swirling around in my brain. Certainly I had heard of it.

"I know what you're thinking. Yes, I'm one of them. But don't assume too much, mister smarty boots. Not all Shibusawas think the same. I know all about you, however."

"Is that so?"

"Yes indeed. Everyone does."

"And how is it that I merit such fame?"

"Ah," she said, shrugging her shoulders. "Not many Americans speak Japanese as well as you. Besides, I hear you are a very good listener. So rare in the Americans, who seem to be fond of their own voices."

"That is true, regrettably," I said.

She then suddenly sat up and seized my wrist, baffling me with her intention. Then she pulled back my shirtsleeve just enough to make my wristwatch visible.

"Oh dear me. I am rather late. I'm always late and my bosses find this so disagreeable. So un-Japanese. *Sou dayo ne*," she said, said using the informal idiom for *isn't that so*? "But I've always run on my own timetable."

I stood when she stood. We shook hands again and bowed.

"Next time you are in the Radio Tokyo building, look me up, Mr. Theodore Lundquist."

I watched her go and found myself regretting that I had turned down her offer of a cigarette even though I had never smoked. I looked at my hands. They were shaking.

I had been ambushed and it wasn't by any destitute waif or government plant.

You would think by that time – I was 26 – I would have had a similar experience. But my shyness and lack of romantic confidence erected a shield against Cupid's arrows. Loves at Ann Arbor developed in predictable stages, starting with intellectual attraction and long, literary conversations. Bedding women was not second nature to me, although I certainly yearned for it and like so many men my age, walked around in a half-libidinous daze.

The pattern altered only once when stationed in Hawaii. Against all odds – during the war men outnumbered women on the islands 100 to one – I discovered the pleasures of being pursued. A Greek-Japanese divorcee ten years my senior, an accountant at the PX, offered me a shockingly short path from coffee to sex. I found her forwardness and lack of inhibitions exciting and a diversion from the work I faced each day at Camp Iroquois. But a deep, burning, and romantic love it was not. It kept my sense of isolation at bay, however. Besides, the whole universe pulsed with irregularity and flux. Settling down and marrying seemed the least sensible thing to do.

Ostensibly, the same conditions existed when I was shipped to Tokyo. Uncertainty fueled by radical change in a tradition-bound society gave one the feeling as being aboard a ship in stormy seas. It's difficult to describe the chaos of post-WW II Japan. A society known for order was anything but: the average Japanese lived on a one thousand calorie per day diet. Sick of deprivation, they rioted for cheaper rice. Unions, long banned, formed and went on strike, clashing with police. The floor under your feet shifted constantly. More than that, you were part of a dynamic responsible for creating these rough waters. Talk about feeling unhinged.

However, I could no longer deny my loneliness; still, stoic fool, I did not pay attention to my growing vulnerability. Susceptibility to big love grew steadily until, like water building behind a weakened dam, it made itself known in an instant.

From that moment at the East Garden of the Imperial Palace, I could think of little else besides this freckled beauty.

With one exception: there was a rumor coming from the legal section of SCAP that the Counter Intelligence Corps based in Kurume, a city on the southern island of Kyushu, had found new evidence concerning the fate of

Peter's downed B-29. I pressed for details but doors were closed at every level, which only made me more suspicious that they'd found something significant.

V
Zenshin
(Advance)

Over the next few days, I could feel my aimlessness start to shift. Anxiety still hung around but I had no more panic attacks. Must be on the right track.

A letter from Alice helped. She wrote it in pencil on a sheet ripped from a spiral notebook. Taut as poetry, not the product of gratuitous scribblings. No crossed out or erased words.

Dear Dad:

You have been on my mind. I know this sounds like fatuous psychobabble, but I can't believe how brave you were the other day to plunge in the way you did.

I suspect the ghosts you mentioned are related, but only marginally.

The sword, obviously still sharp after all these years, is a catalyst for both.

You are not trapped when it comes to the situation with Peter and how he died. The only way out is through. That means real conversation. Not with me. Probably not with Sylvia or a therapist. With other men. I know you walk every day and walk alone. Find a partner to walk the miles. Something might happen. Take that risk.

Dealing with Noriko's ghost requires a different approach, some sort of action. Merely giving the sword away won't do it, either, not if you're seeking resolution and peaceful slumbers. That's like kneeling in church hoping that mere prayer in an edifice that favors forgiveness will absolve you of sins. I find it rarely leads to meaningful results, especially with lapsed Lutherans like you. You've always been a plodder, Dad, a relentless plodder.

After reading that letter, I resolved to find out if Noriko was still alive. If I was going to give the sword to anyone, it was to her.

When I retired, I pledged I would cease this business of nosing into her life. It was easier than I thought. When you're no longer sitting at a computer that allows you to access to the lives of others, it's not so hard to give up the behavior. It's like giving up smoking if you suddenly have no access to tobacco.

Still, the Noriko dreams kept coming.

A part of me hoped that my search for Noriko would come to naught, that I could say: *I tried to find her, tried to do the right thing but, alas, too much time had passed.*

Advancing technology and a lifetime of priding myself in research skills demolished this excuse. I was modestly proud that I did not make a few phone calls to friends at my old firm and ask them for a favor. Instead, I subscribed to an on-line research service; it was expensive, even for a 90-day period, the shortest time they offered, and I wondered if it was worth the trouble. Sylvia didn't much care for it because using the program meant monopolizing our phone line.

Since I hadn't looked into Noriko's life for ten years, and I assumed that even the best commercial research software would be inferior to what I was accustomed to in my professional life; I figured it would take me at least a few weeks to find Noriko.

I had not been paying attention. Technology had made leaps and bounds since I retired, giving me access to information and data that back in my working days would have been the province of the military or research universities.

My brain, sclerotic with age, struggled in learning the new software but as Alice correctly observed. I'm a plodder. What I'm saying is that I found Noriko in less than two days. I knew her married name: Noriko Tomonosuke. The name stuck because I recalled the Tomonosuke name from my class on Japanese military history. Takashima Tomonosuke was a viscount who became the Japanese minister of war in the 1880s. I figured out he was Noriko's husband's grandfather. Like marries like.

###

It was said that the residents of Koningsburg could set their clocks by the regularity of the daily walks by their famous native son, Immanuel Kant. When I first read that I thought such regularity improbable and daffy. Not so now. Day after day, my routine varies little. It's a comforting monotony. I arise each day at 5:30 – later during the dark days of winter – and take a long walk with Diego then I indulge in my one of last vestiges of my time in Tokyo: I soak in a deep bath. I've had a deep Japanese style tub installed in every home I've lived in, including San Paolo and Helsinki. Traditionally, Japanese take a hot bath at the end of the day but I need the heat to help relax my bad back and leg muscles after my walk.

It's a vastly underrated way to start the day, sinking into barely tolerable hot water. I recommend it to everyone over 65. Sometimes I cut my walk short just so I can feel the pleasure, almost the way in my younger years I would shove off chores and obligations if Sylvia had hinted she was ready for a roll in the hay.

Occasionally, however, this sensation carries a bittersweet memory: Noriko and I spent many hours soaking together. I don't I recall this every time, of course, but the memory comes often enough.

The telephone rang as I was getting out of the tub. Sylvia answered. I didn't have my hearing aids in; only muffled bits and snippets reached my ears, although I could tell she was speaking in half Portuguese and half English. Must be Nick. The timing was right. Sao Tome and Principe is eight hours ahead of Flagstaff. Then I heard the register of Sylvia's voice change and knew she was talking to one of our granddaughters. The distance between us and our grandchildren in Sao Tome and Principe constitutes the sole regret of us living in Flagstaff. Sylvia has twice flown there to visit. She went alone, which pained me, but I can no longer tolerate flights longer than four or five hours.

I had finished toweling off and managed to pull on my shirt and stumble into my underwear when Sylvia walked in, phone outstretched in her hand, face serious.

"Nick," she said, looking at me. "And you're definitely t-o-o thin."

After a few niceties, Nick launched into the reason for the call.

"Mom told me you've got an old sword you want to return to Japan. Is that right?"

"It is."

"Where are you going with this sword once you get to Japan? Whose the recipient?"

"The rightful owners," I said.

"Are they still alive?"

"I think so," I lied. I did not want Nick prying into anything concerning Noriko. I felt my annoyance with Sylvia's telling Nick about the sword returning. "I'm working on it."

"You want some help locating the person?"

"No, thanks. I'm pretty sure I've still got the necessary resources to find her."

"It's a *her*? asked Nick. "Well. You took this sword from a woman? Interesting."

I felt like yelping like Diego when I've stepped on his toe. "It's a convoluted tale, Nick. Sometime I'll tell you about it."

There was a silence and I could tell Nick was deciding whether to push me or let the matter go. He had his mother's penchant for details and questions.

I heard a quick sigh of resolution and I knew he would give me a pass but he wasn't finished. "All right, Dad, but I've looked into the business of returning samurai swords to Japan. They've changed the rules. They did it years ago actually but you can definitely do it. There's a ton of paperwork. The Japanese government wants to know the circumstances of its removal from the country.

They also want to know exactly, right down the street address, where the sword is going once you enter the country. Furthermore, I can tell you right now it's a lot easier to simply ship the sword to Japan than it is to go there in person. Why don't you deploy that action versus enduring the hassle of delivering the sword yourself? Makes a lot more sense for an eighty-year-old man. Know what I mean? Either way, you sure you don't want my assistance?"

"I still think I'm OK. Thanks, though. I'll let you know if I need any help."

A half cough, half sigh told me he wasn't quite going to let me off the hook. "OK, Dad. But why don't I email you the particulars?"

"That would be helpful."

Satisfied he had made some headway against a stubborn old man, Nick then asked me if I wanted to speak to my granddaughters. Relieved, I said I'd be delighted. In the back of my mind, however, I realized returning the sword would be more complicated than I thought.

But it wasn't, really. Nicholas was just being his tight-assed state department self. I printed out the information that Nicholas sent me and realized that if there were difficulties, they would appear after I arrived in Japan. I would declare the sword. It would then be inspected by the port police and, if all went well, I would be issued a temporary import permit. This would allow me to travel with the sword in Japan. But not to Noriko's house. That would be too simple. Rather I would be obliged to appear at the Education Board of Kyoto prefecture before a group called a *Shinsa*, or sword evaluation committee. This requirement reminded me that everything of supreme importance in Japan is somehow connected to education.

That afternoon when Sylvia took Diego to have a doggie shampoo and nails trimmed, I stretched out on the living room couch for my mandatory afternoon nap. My hand is steadier and mind clearest after I sleep. But before eased myself down, I printed out Noriko's address from the computer. Then I located a single piece of good writing paper of high rag content, a vintage Tsuchida lacquer eyedropper fountain pen (a gift from Noriko), and an anthology of Kamakura Period poetry. I loaded the pen with fresh ink and set everything on my desk. I had in mind several poems written by the monk poet, Saigyō, that I wanted to use to transmit my situation to Noriko.

I drifted off only for a short while. When I awoke, I immediately knew which poem to use. I did not need to open my anthology and instead wrote from memory:

Did I ever imagine
I would make this pass again
in my old age?
Such is life!
Sayononake Mountain.

I have something, my dear Noriko, of yours that I must return, something that needs to be delivered in person.

Tanomu Yo (which meant: I beg your indulgence)

Noppo

I folded the letter and stuck it in a cheap envelope, a temporary protective measure before I ventured to the FedEx office in the morning.

I often see other walkers in the morning. They come in three categories: couples, usually older; small groups of women, carrying on intense conversations they can't have with their husbands; and single men, all of them at least middle aged. I never see any man under 30 out walking. Instead, he's running. I can relate. Since high school, I began each day with a run. I loved it but also paid the price. About 15 years ago surgeons fused my lower vertebra, shot from years of impact.

This morning, letter to Noriko in hand, I ran into Walter. He's roughly my age, if not a few years younger, and sticks to the vicinity around Bushmaster Park. He's got the same build as I, tall and thin, and wears a brace on his right knee.

I try and vary my walking routine and route. Walter hasn't changed his walking pattern since I first saw him.

He wears the same outfits changing them for weather conditions, of course, and even then they tend to be the same articles of clothing for every season. In that way, I'm the same. I'm still wearing the same training pants I did when I was 70. Only my shoes change.

Walter has a wary, wiry, nervous Weimaraner bitch named Queeny. She's always kept on a leash. I regularly violate leash laws with Diego, mostly because we've trained him to heal unless we tell him it's OK to roam.

Since moving to Flagstaff, I haven't sought out new male friends. Haven't even tried. Age affirms my solitary nature. I'm happy with my books, music, and gardening. Plus, face it: most old men are a pain in the ass. All they want to do it hear themselves talk and it's mostly about how the world is going to hell. Who needs that? This lack of new acquaintances worries Sylvia but she's given up encouraging me to socialize more.

Sometimes Walter and I stop and shoot the breeze; it tends to be a superficial conversation about weather or dogs or sometimes sports. The only sport I follow is college football, a leftover from when Peter played for the University of Idaho. Walter follows all team sports, in particular pro football and hockey. So usually we just say good morning and wave and keep on our merry way.

One bond between us, however: we both have military experience, although Walter made it his career, Air Force. More importantly, we both had older brothers who served in Japanese POW camps, although Peter's demise didn't occur in a camp, per se. Walt doesn't know the full details but he's aware that Peter died at the hands of the Japanese.

His brother was captured towards the end of the war but still the four months he served in Singapore was no picnic. Walter said his brother was never the same after that, even though he received no especially ill treatment except starvation rations.

"When he came out his uniform hung off his frame like a scarecrow. Until the day he died, he kept a room in his basement full of canned food and water," Walter had told me.

Walt's also a reader, a welcome relief in that most men our age idea of literary adventurism means turning off Fox News for five minutes and scanning the front page of *USA Today*. Walt has a limited venue, however, mostly history, especially military history. He considers himself quite an expert. At times he bored me witless with his armchair analysis of battles. Still, I admire his curiosity and willingness to learn.

This morning, I found Walter sitting on a bench, his Weimaraner pacing, unhappy about her stationary situation. Walter was not too sunny, either. His knee was acting up. The morning stroll, he said curtly, was about to be cut short.

"Take a load off," he said, gesturing towards a space on the bench. "What's new?"

Diego and Queeny sniffed each other, both stubby tails vibrating, then the Weimaraner feigned disinterest. She wanted to get moving.

I was about retreat into the standard *not much* routine but I thought about Alice's admonition to talk with men about what happen to Peter. I couldn't just launch into it, though. I eased into the topic.

"I'm doing all right. But I'm in the middle of sorting out kind of a delicate subject."

"Oh," he said, immediately thinking it might be interesting, even though it probably wasn't about sports. "How delicate?"

"Well, you know I served in occupied Japan for a few years."

"Right. For MacArthur."

I paused, thinking this conversation was probably a bad idea. Then I said,

"That's right," I said, and then clammed up, pessimism gaining the upper hand.

"Well," said Walt impatiently. "What happened?"

Too late to turn back.

"I got tangled up with a woman. I mean, really involved."

"Like getting married?" Walter asked. "A Japanese woman, I take it."

"Yes. That was the plan. Get hitched and move to California. Some place around San Francisco or maybe San Diego."

"And?"

"She left me about two months before my commission expired."

Walter bowed his head in dismay, looked at the ground. "Sheesh," he said.

"Didn't take the news too well. In fact, I got so pissed I broke into her apartment and stole a family sword."

This got Walter's attention.

"No shit?"

"No shit and I'm not very proud of it. I'm even less proud of what I did afterwards. I should have returned it but I didn't."

As I feared, Walter didn't take the inquisitive route. Nor did he wait for more details. Instead, he immediately offered justification. "Oh, hell, Ted. Lots of boys came home with swords. Thousands of them. I wouldn't lose much sleep over your actions."

"That was different. Those swords came from repositories, most of them former imperial arsenals. Anybody in uniform could go in there and pick one out."

"And where did those arsenals get those swords?" he asked, messaging his knee and using an inflection that told me he knew the answer. He just wanted me to say it.

"From people's homes."

"Exactly. Our boys or the Aussies confiscated them. And in my book, confiscation is just another word for theft. Instead of stealing when they weren't looking, we took them right in front of their eyes. We made them bring those swords to their front door. It was a silly-ass policy, if you ask me, and a waste of time. What were the Japs going to do? Rise up wielding ancient weapons? Shit. I approve of the psychological aspect, though."

"Which was?"

Walt looked at me, somewhat surprised that I would ask the question.

"Humiliation, Ted. We were stripping them of something that represented honor and strength, the symbol of the samurai and clan loyalty. In my book, that was essential."

So much for the considered wisdom of an armchair military historian.

"But Walt, the Japanese were utterly defeated. Completely. You just said as much yourself. When the emperor said they must bear the unbearable, they did it. End of story. The whole time I was in Japan, I never met any Japanese who even hinted they were going to rekindle the flame of the Japanese empire."

Walt shook his head. "That's not what I think. I think that flame finally got extinguished because we broke their pride with the Fat Boy and kept on breaking it, in a nicer way, of course, like taking their symbols of power and re-writing their constitution. Ted, I was reading the other day that they found another Jap infantryman hiding away on some isolated atoll, refusing to surrender. That's over fifty years after the end of the damned war. The Japanese may be smart and organized but they're also sheep and suckers for nationalistic ideology."

I was about to protest but then I saw Walt look away, perhaps regretting his words. Maybe he would understand my dilemma, which is the reaction I wanted. He stroked the twitching Queeny. "I don't know, Ted. Maybe you're right. Are you seriously thinking about returning the sword?"

"I'm trying to arrange it right now."

Walt shook his head and got up off the bench. "You want my opinion? I'd never give that sword back to that woman or her family. Never in a million years. Not after what they did to our POWs. Think of what they did to your brother. Does that really make you want to return the sword? The woman doesn't deserve to reclaim it."

"But she wasn't related to that action."

"Listen to me, Ted. I've read about this. We got some of those war criminals, but in 1952, that goddamn treaty we signed with the Japanese government ended military tribunals. Hundreds of war criminals skated. A hall pass on a grand scale. Shirō Ishii. That name ring a bell?"

Did it ever. Ishii was the Japanese doctor in charge of the infamous 731 unit in Manchuria that performed biological experiments on prisoners, mostly Chinese.

"It does."

"Yeah, well, then you know MacArthur and the brass granted immunity to that twisted bastard."

"I was working for the SCAP at the time. I watched the whole Ishii drama unfold."

"Then good God, my friend," he said in mild exasperation. "You, of all people, should know the Japs didn't pay a fraction of what they owed the rest of the world, especially us Yanks. They made their bed. Now they've got to sleep in it. Now we buy their cars and computers and cameras every other damned thing."

Walt untied Queeny. "My fucking knee is killing me. Better go ice it and chuck down some ibuprofen. I hate that stuff. Gives me heartburn for a week. I need to bite the bullet and get this knee replaced. See you 'round. And stop being such a goody-goody."

VI
Pigskin and the Orient

Living in Pocatello, Japan retained a distant but prominent place in my solar system, a Venus of interests, far away but always shining bright. It even came up when playing football with Peter, who had been bitten by the pigskin bug. He constantly harassed me into two-man scrimmages. I was useless. Not only was I uninterested and uncoordinated but I had inherited my father's slight, willowy build. My nickname was Goose. When Peter hit me, I folded like a rag, flopping to earth. I could never anticipate his moves, no matter how many times he gave me tips on how to do so.

"He's not Japanese, Peter, he's Chinese."

This bit of ethnographic erudition came as I lay groaning on the grass, having been firmly planted there by my brother.

He tucked the football under one arm, shaded his eyes and looked at me. "What?"

I had been trying to convince Peter to halt this torture. I had been reduced to bribery, offering to buy him a hamburger at the Metropolitan Restaurant downtown.

"You mean the place run by that old Jap?," he had asked.

"The man who runs the Metropolitan is Chinese, not Japanese."

Peter tossed the football back and forth from hand to hand, not looking at it, confident in even the smallest trajectory. "How do you know?

I lifted my head. "Mrs. Clonnenburg told us in history class. She also said he's selling the restaurant and taking his money back to China. The only problem is, she says, there's no China to go back to. China she, says, has been carved up like a melon and the Japanese are doing most of the carving."

"OK enough lessons for the day, school marm. C'mon, Goose, go out for a pass, would ya? Just one more."

"You said the last play was the final one of the day."

"Yeah, I've been reading about those Japs in the Tribune," he said. "But they sure make good-looking girls. Those Takeda sisters. I'd like to go for a roll in the alfalfa with one of them." He grinned wolfishly.

He said this partly to get a rise out me. He knew I had a crush on Sumi Takeda. "C'mon," he said, walking over to me and pulling me up. "One more scrimmage. Promise. I'll even play on the offensive. Last one. All you gotta do is tackle me before I get to Pa's raspberry break."

There was no Pop Warner football in 1930s Idaho, just rough and tumble pick-up games played in the dirt. The teams, such as they were, were usually made up of the sons of the sons of the British Empire and Italians toughs. Although quick and nimble, my brother's size worked against him until he had his growth spurt. He took lumps and not all of them associated with the rawness of the game. But Peter was never one to take abuse and older players learned he gave as good as he got. He regularly came home with black eyes and swollen lips.

My father had remarried. Peter's pummelings racked our stepmother with worry. She pleaded with my father to forbid Peter from playing football. He did no such thing. My father was wise enough, probably deeply relieved, to see that Peter had finally found an outlet for his energy. Besides, scrimmages held outside the backyard meant that my father's precious currant, gooseberry, jostaberry and – in particular – lingonberry – plants were in less danger. He merely bought his son a leather helmet and a pair of padded pants, a gift that engendered acute envy in me.

"I'll even spring for the burger," he said. "I'll give that Chinaman one more quarter so he can go back to China and live like a king."

"No kings in China. They have emperors. Or they used to."

Peter gave the distinction no notice. He was strolling to the east side of our terraced lawn, ready to sprint to the cane break on the other side, taunting me to stop him.

Two months later, I got frog-marched to the back lawn no more. Peter entered high school, joined the football team, and became the most storied player in Pocatello history.

His status gave him immunity in a town craving for good news and a hero. Like daring Achilles of yore, Peter's good looks and achievements gave him a hall pass on his bad behavior: poor grades – which humiliated my father – taking stranger's cars for joyrides, visiting a brothel, stealing a bottle of ouzo from the backroom of a Greek bakery, and brawling with anyone stupid enough to challenge him.

###

Southern Idaho tried to pretend it was stronger than the sullied outside world. But the corset of the Depression squeezed the life out of the region. By the summer of 1936 almost everyone had exhausted their resources. Yet the hardships largely passed me by. Not only had my father stayed employed, he'd left extension for a teaching position at Idaho Technical Institute, now called University of Idaho, Southern Branch.

The University of Idaho gave Peter a full athletic scholarship. The summer before he left for Moscow, he also acquired a summer job at Idaho Iron and Steel. It paid $5.00 per day, a working wage in the Depression. My father disapproved, saying that such a position should go to married man with a family to feed. Yet the owner of the scrapyard, a major high school football booster, felt otherwise.

The work was hard. He was a breaker, taking down old cars. Peter's already muscular frame rippled like a moving cordwood.

"You'll never guess what came in the yard today, Goose."

"What?"

"An old steam locomotive. It was built in fucking 1884. That's 15 years older than Pop. It came down the tracks on its own power although it was blowing steam all over. Groaning like an old whore. It was pulling another locomotive, only this one wasn't in operating order."

"What are they going to do with them?" I asked.

"What do you think? Same as we do everything else. Cut 'em up with the torch and send the pieces to Portland."

"What happens to them then?"

"Gets shipped to Tokyo. Japs are so desperate for steel they go all the way to Pocatello fucking Idaho to get it. Biggest importers of scrap steel in world. Boss says the Japs are keeping him in business."

I went to the library to check on my brother's assertion about Japan and scrap steel. He was right. I stared at the map of Japan: 145,000 square miles, about the size Idaho's neighbor: Montana. I tried to imagine Montana being the biggest importer of scrap steel in the world. I'd been through the state twice, once by car and once by train, to visit relatives. All I saw was trees, field upon field of wheat, and prairie. What would that world look like with steel mills?

My projected future plans took a sharp deviation the next year. I had assumed that I was to receive a college education at home, at least the first two years as Idaho Southern was still a junior college. As the child of a faculty member, tuition was practically free; I could live at home. No one had ever given me the idea I had other options.

One Friday afternoon the telephone rang. My stepmother answered. I was in my bedroom, reading. She called from the bottom of the stairs. "Theodore. It's for you. It's man – a Mr. Stevens – from the admission's office at the University of Idaho," she said and gave me a look of curiosity and suspicion as I came down, as if I were responsible for this call.

Mr. Stevens told me that he was visiting from Moscow and wondered if I could spare a few minutes. If so, would it be all right if he paid me a personal call? In fact, would it be too much of an imposition if he showed up tomorrow morning? I was both flattered and flabbergasted. When he arrived, I was furthermore impressed that while polite and courteous to my father and stepmother, this Mr. Stevens made it clear that I was the one he wanted to talk to. Alone.

He didn't look like an academic. No tweed jacket or bow tie. He rather dressed like my father except his suit was in better condition. We took a stroll on the path besides the river. I managed to ask how I had come his attention. Was Peter behind this, I wanted to know? To the contrary, Mr. Stevens assured me. A certain faculty member at Pocatello High had written to the admission's office to recommend me. I knew who that was: Mrs. Clonnenburg, my beloved history teacher. Her brother had been a Rhodes scholar and she admired – no, worshiped – academic prowess. Mr. Stevens had then called our high school principal who spoke glowingly of my straight A report card.

"He says you have an interest in Asia. Is that true?"

"Yes."

"Any particular country?"

"I find Japan pretty fascinating. Been taking a lot of books about that country out of the library."

"I see. Have you ever thought about studying the Japanese language? Goethe once said that he who knows no foreign language does not know his own."

Never heard of Goethe but I was suitably impressed, also intimidated. "I don't know, Mr. Stevens. It seems like it would be a difficult language to learn."

"Maybe," said Mr. Stevens. "But don't sell yourself short."

In a bit of a backhanded compliment to my brother, he added, "A university, a true university, needs more than good athletes, Ted. It needs scholars, like you. We need students interested in the world outside of Idaho. We'd like to offer you a full scholarship to Moscow."

Mr. Stevens didn't ask for a commitment, probably because he saw I was so stunned I couldn't utter a syllable. He merely asked that I consider this scholarship like there were others coming my way, of which there were none. He urged me to talk it over with my parents and offered to pay the bus fare for a visit. I liked the fact that he didn't say, *next time you're up watching your brother play football, stop by the admission's office*. My brain was going to pay the freight. He made me feel awfully important and plans for attending my hometown college disappeared.

  The visit did not sit well with my father. He made perfunctory and pleasant comments about my diligence being rewarded. But Mr. Steven's overture stirred up something. I suspect numerous agents at work: not only did my father not want me to be a Vandal, he did not want me to again live in my brother's shadow. For the past five years, Peter's pigskin prowess eclipsed all. Reporters and football supporters fawned over him. Everywhere we went: the movies or in a restaurant, people came up to us to talk about Peter's athletic feats on the Vandal football field, following his progress with almost religious fervor.

  Mr. Stevens's visit awakened in my father the thought that he was possibly guilty of benign neglect. I don't know this for sure. Talking about emotions was nearly impossible for my father. Instead, he hid in his study and read, which he did more than usual after Mr. Stevens's visit.

  A few weeks later, my father stunned me by announcing at the dinner table that he and I were having Thanksgiving at his brother's house in Traverse City, Michigan. My stepmother and Peter were going to Twin Falls to celebrate this national day of overeating with my stepmother's people. Any Italian will tell you that Thanksgiving, not Christmas or Columbus Day is the most sacred American holiday. I did not discover that yes, we were going to cherry tree-lined streets of

Traverse City, but Ann Arbor, home to the University of Michigan, was our first stop.

VII

Yokubo
(Desire)

I dipped down the steps and brushed through the three-part valence curtain at the door to my favorite *izakaya*, located about three blocks from Dai Ichi. I had discovered the gem just by chance and took an instant liking to its atmosphere. Quaint, ancient, dark, and compact, it didn't open until the early afternoon and closed in the small hours of the morning.

SCAP had instituted all nature of rules preventing fraternization between occupying forces and Japanese citizens, particularly in relationship to patronizing restaurants, bars, and brothels. It was an exercise in wishful thinking, ignored from the start, particularly by yours truly, although I stayed clear of geishas and what I considered dicey female company. It wasn't as if I wasn't interested. I was just shy and chicken.

Besides, I had developed what I considered my first real friendship in Japan: Mrs. Ogawa, a widow in her mid-60s. It was her bar and besides the cook, her nephew, she was the sole employee. She would glide between her seat in back of the bar to the other parts of the establishment: a small nook with a low table that would fit four people and a single room with tatami mats that was separated from the rest of the bar by a sliding door. Through observing her manners and small talk, I learned invaluable lessons in Japanese etiquette. She adopted me, in a way, and because the Japanese have such difficulty pronouncing the "L's," – Lundquist always came out, *Runquist* – Mrs. Ogawa just called me Teddy, the only Japanese – besides Noriko – to recognized the diminutive of Theodore.

I discovered this establishment to be a favored hideout for many corporate titans and political poobahs – not to mention employees of the Imperial household. It was the place to be unseen. Mrs. Ogawa was a repository of high-octane gossip and not a little wisdom.

Although she knew some English and occasionally wanted to keep up her marginal fluency, we spoke in Japanese.

I sat ruminating about my date with Noriko – our first – while Mrs. Ogawa brought me a hot towel then tended my sake cup.

"Last time you were here, you had a friend, Teddy," she said.

"Yes."

"I've never seen you in here with a girl. You mostly drink by yourself. She a special friend?"

"We don't know yet."

"What is her name?"

"Noriko."

"Most Japanese have a surname, Teddy."

"Shibusawa."

Mrs. Ogawa gently – almost imperceptivity – raised her eyebrows. A little shiver of excitement went through my body. She knew something about Noriko or something about her family.

"Is that so?" was all she said and poured me another cup of house sake and pushed a bowl of *hiyayakko*, cold tofu covered with chopped green onions and dried tuna flakes and soy, toward me. Then she moved away to take care of something in the kitchen.

Noriko and I had sneaked out of offices early, even though were we both buried in obligations. For this occasion, I wanted to secure the privacy of the low table in the nook. Noriko was only marginally late. Her wardrobe had changed little from our last meeting. Different blouse. Different skirt although plain as the last. Same shoes. If she was rich, she wasn't spending her money on clothes. She was, however, wearing perfume. Noriko looked around as she knelt down at the table. "I must say, I have never been here," she said, "How did you find it?"

"Stumbled upon it the first week I was here. Walking back to the hotel where I live."

"Nobody showed it to you?"

I shook my head.

"You're not to supposed to be in places like this."

"I know. I'm not supposed to be associating with the likes you, either. What are they going to do? Throw me in the brig? What would they do without their chief translator and Man Friday?"

Noriko's freckled nose crinkled in pleasure at the recognized the name. "Robinson Crusoe," she said. "You're a naughty man, though, disobeying orders."

"I'm not so bad, really."

"And do you like this place? Why do you find so compelling?"

"Not much compelling as it is comforting."

She looked at me quizzically: "Comfort?"

"It's reassuring that places like this survived. It represents a kind of Japanese tradition that I was afraid would be gone after war. I like its, its *Japaneseness* as Lafcadio Hearn would say: it serves beer and sake only, not godawful Japanese scotch or Russian vodka. While it also serves food, the menu is limited and doesn't seem to change much."

Noriko's eyes were upon me. "You, Theodore, have a traditionalist streak in you." It was almost an accusation.

"I thought you knew everything about me," I said. "That's what you said last week."

"Well," she said, tilting her head coyly. "Not everything."

"No? Let's hear my resume," challenging her and expecting a retreat. It did not come. She took out a cigarette and lit it herself. I reminded myself I needed to buy a lighter.

"OK. If I must. You were born in the potato state, have a brother who was lost in the war, went to the University of Michigan, took a commission in the Army, some sort of intelligence branch, ended up in Hawaii where you interrogated prisoners. At the end of the war, you ended up stationed with Allied Command in Tokyo. How did I do?"

She had missed lots, of course, but she knew enough about me that maybe she *was* a government paid snoop. Besides, the blanks might be narrative of omission. Noriko probably knew more but didn't want to reveal all. Yet her answer was an admission she had taken the time to do some digging on me. I was more than just a passing curiosity for Noriko. My heart pounded like a schoolboy.

"Not bad," I said and before I could say, "tell me about your relationship to England," Mrs. Ogawa showed up with our tray.

I had chosen a bottle of top-shelf sake for the occasion, good enough that it could have been served cold. Yet the heavy humidity of the day gave one a dank feeling down to the bone. Better hot than cold. Mrs. Ogawa had heated up the sake to the perfect degree, just above body temperature, and served it in a lovely vintage gray ceramic *tokkuri*, or sake vessel, decorated with kanji. It came with matching cups. When the tray arrived, Mrs. Ogawa knelt. She and Noriko gave a millisecond glance that must have transmitted, among other things – god knows what – that Noriko would pour, not our hostess. Noriko was in charge. Mrs. Ogawa got up, gave a short bow, then returned to the bar.

Mrs. Ogawa had wrapped the tokkuri snuggly in a white, ironed cotton towel. Noriko grasped the tokkuri with both hands, like she was handling some sort of sacred object, palm facing slightly downward and lifted it off the tray, my cue to hold my cup in the palm of my hand and steady it with two fingers from my other hand.

She filled the cup almost to the brim; it's poor form to stint on sake. Yet knowing that I would have to set my cup down and pour for her, Noriko left a little space at the top of the cup so I wouldn't spill. She replaced the tokkuri on the tray, then waited until I had taken up the vessel with both hands before lifting her cup to me, tilted ever so slightly, meaning she wanted the cup filled to the exact level as mine. She waited until I had set down the tokkuri on the tray before looking at me.

We simultaneously took a small sip, the aroma already rising up our noses, savoring the subdued fruitiness.

We did not say *kampai*.

We set our cups down at the same time with a quiet clack. It was as if we had done the ritual a thousand times together.

She then gently pulled the cotton towel away from the tokkuri, not all the way, just enough for us to see the kanji characters written on the ceramic. I bent my head forward.

Noriko looked at me quizzically, not having to ask the question: do you know what that says?

I studied the kanji for a moment, trying to forge the characters an idiom. I knew the last three characters: *botan-yuki*: snowflakes as large as a peony blossom. And while I recognized the first characters of the phrase, I couldn't forge them into a coherent phrase, although it was something about eating heavily in the fall. But I felt an urge to impress.

"Between harvest and snow?" I guessed.

"Very good, gaijin," she said, approvingly. "Very good. It refers to the time between when fruit ripens and when the snow starts falling in big flakes."

"So it is about taking advantage of the fruit harvest?"

"Yes but only partially. It's about developing our appetites, all our appetites, when something ripens. For as we well know, desires come and go. But because these characters are painted on a tokkuri, we have to put the meaning in context. It's about the time when we begin making sake in Japan, the season that's about to start right now. To me, it's one of the most romantic seasons of the year. To hell with spring and cherry blossoms, I say. It's sake, lush fruit, and beautiful leaves that I love."

VIII

The Flame Jumps the Fireline

My father's parting gift, which he handed me at the Pocatello train station, was a copy of *Plutarch's Lives*. He had bookmarked the page that contained one of the Greek's most famous maxims: *The mind is not a vessel to be filled but a fire to be kindled.* The University of Michigan's out-of-state tuition had strained the family's budget. My father knew I was aware of this burden. The gift of Plutarch was his way of saying: that doesn't matter. Go explore.

I did and yet discovered that some new doors cannot be closed again. The accumulation of knowledge, at the right time and place, draws attention from the outside. Turning inward as an escape often proves futile.

To paraphrase Emily Dickinson, I had no time to stop for war, so it kindly stopped for me. It was the type of fall day that colleges like to use in recruitment brochures: Indian summer October, mid-60s, maple and oak leaves skittering about the pavement in a slight breeze. Students were still wearing short-sleeve shirts and shorts, going on about the upcoming football game against Ohio State. I myself was chatting up a redhead who was wearing a wonderfully skimpy skirt. As we came out of the Union Building I noticed a man in Army officer's uniform holding a briefcase, looking directly at us. My stomach did a little flip. He motioned with his head for me to come to him, like he was a buddy I'd known for a long time. I excused myself from the girl.

"Theodore Lundquist?" he asked.

"Yes."

He stuck out a hand. "Pleased to meet you. Captain Ames Carlson. You have a minute?"

I felt a surge of anxiety but also excitement. There were rumors that the Army intelligence was prowling about universities with Japanese programs.

"Sure."

"Terrific. Why don't we take a seat over there?" he said, pointing toward a bench under a red oak tree.

When we were seated, he said, "your department head said that of all the students studying Japanese history and literature, you had the most advanced degree of comprehension, both in spoken and in particular written Japanese."

I think I blushed. "Well, that was kind of Dr. Horn."

He startled me by speaking in Japanese. "An act of kindness, perhaps. But is it true?"

I was so flustered I didn't know what to say. Understood the words but couldn't formulate a reply. Finally, I blurted out, *tabun*, or maybe so.

Captain Carlson unsnapped his briefcase and withdrew a small, dark red booklet with a paper cover. He handed it to me. It was a Japanese Imperial Army manual on tank maneuver and strategy.

I opened to the frontispiece. "Read, please, out loud. That and a paragraph from the introduction, if you can," said Captain Carlson in a tone that did not carry much ambiguity. It just so happened that I was studying an ancient Japanese treatise on battles. I managed to stumble through the assignment but noted, with some pride, that there were only a few characters I not recognize.

Captain Carlson took the book back. "Not bad," he said in Japanese, as he tucked the book back in briefcase. Then he turned his gaze upon me.

"Mr. Lundquist, I'm recruiting candidates for an accelerated Japanese language learning program. I'm with MIS, the Military Intelligence Service. Ever heard of us?"

"Yes, I think so."

"Do you know how many people in the United States, those of non-Japanese ancestry, who speak Japanese with any degree of fluency?

"No, sir. I understand it's not all that many."

"Our best estimates are under 50 in the entire US. That's it. If we include Nisei, the ones who can really understand the full spectrum of the language, both written and spoken, the number goes up to about 100. Maybe."

After making sure we had direct eye contact, he said, "Mr. Lundquist. I'll come right to the point. The United States is concerned about the martial ambitions of Japan. We think some sort of conflict is inevitable and we, my friend, are perilously behind in preparation. Would you consider applying for a commission in the MIS?"

This proposal left me nearly speechless. All I could utter was something witty, like, "gosh."

Captain Carlson gave a pained but sympathetic smile. "Don't worry. You don't have to make any commitments right now. Besides, all I'm offering is an invitation. There's a lot of hoops to jump through before we'd grant a commission."

"When would this application process start? I'm assuming after I graduate in December."

Captain Carlson shook his head. "The process, if you're interested, starts the day after tomorrow. Takes place over at the law school. We'd like you to come to the basement of the Legal Research Building. Room 128. 8:00 AM. We'll put you through a series of test. You won't be alone. In fact, I think you'll probably recognize everyone who shows up."

"What happens if I pass these tests?"

"We'll talk about that later. But, if you pass muster and agree to what comes next, your days at Ann Arbor will come to an end."

"What about my degree?"

"Your department head said you're only five credits short of a bachelors. Is that correct?"

"Yes sir, it is."

"Close enough. And when it comes to receiving your piece of parchment, the university said that if you accept a commission, the degree is yours."

"Dr. Horn said that?"

"No, the dean of the college of arts and sciences said that."

Two days later I made my way to the basement of the Legal Research Building. Captain Carlson was right. I knew almost everybody in that room, every occidental that is, from the Oriental Studies department. There were also about five Nisei, none of whom I recognized. For six hours, Captain Carlson and a Japanese man named Mr. Mori plumbed our knowledge of written and spoken Japanese, including comprehension. There was no place to hide as they weeded out the less proficient in public. Captain Carlson would slap a Japanese military manual or newspaper down on your desk and ask you read it out loud, then translate. Mr. Mori would arbitrarily choose then ask us to give our opinion, in Japanese, on current trends in Japanese society. If you managed to stumble through, he would ask follow up questions. There was also a written exam. By the end of the day, my head felt like it had been in a vice. I was sure I'd failed everything. But out of the seventeen candidates who showed up, I was part of three who remained and the only non-Nisei. All three of us had been accepted into the new Military Intelligence Service Language School in San Francisco.

The Army gave us five days to make up our minds. Pending a few other tests and interviews I must pass, I was offered a commission. I called my parents. They listened then my father spoke, his voice carrying both worry and latent approval, but mostly worry. He may have been conflict avoidant but, much to his credit, he spoke up at critical times. "It's going to be exciting but you're not going to have many options," he said. Thinking about my perfectionist predilection for putting off decisions until in possession of what I considered was all the necessary information, my father scripted my future in scientist's terms: "Try and make the best decisions you can with limited data."

Peter was less hesitant. He was 23 at the time and had parlayed his reputation as a football star into working as a potash salesman for the JR Simplot corporation. He'd written me how easy it was to bamboozle clients into contracts using his tales of glory as a Vandal's quarterback. He was, he said, raking in the dough and just bought a Ford Super Deluxe Coup in cash.

"Oh, hell yes, Goose. I'd take that offer and run with it. You better believe if the Japs make trouble, I'm coming in right behind you."

####

The news froze my tongue to the top of my mouth and my feet to the phone booth floor: Peter had washed out of the Navy's program for training future officers, the

Midshipmen's School at Northwestern. I wasn't so much shocked that he had not made it. In fact, when Peter had called me and said he wanted to be a Navy pilot and he was going after a commission, my first thought was: You'll never survive. Not only was a commission a five-to-seven-year commitment, but Peter's insouciant, don't-give-a-damn personality was bound to clash in a command and control culture.

What rattled me was the reason for his dismissal.

"They said it was an integrity violation," said my father so quietly I could barely hear him.

"A what?"

There was a silence then my father said, "We got a letter that said Peter had been caught cheating on a test, a math test," said my father in a voice he used when trying not to betray any emotion. "It was apparently the second violation, although the evidence of the first offense was somewhat murky and they let him stay. Not this time."

I recall being more concerned for my father's well-being than mine. My father valued humility and his eldest son had little. He knew Peter had gotten away with murder most of his life and, if the world made any sense, his son's day of reckoning would arrive. I sensed my father was relieved that humbleness had been forced on my brother, although the means for achieving this new station was excruciating. My father had a stoic's sense of honor, not to mention being an academic; to have a son expelled for cheating cut him to the bone. He never spoke of it again.

Still, I couldn't imagine that the Navy wasn't reluctant to see my brother go. People followed Peter around like the pied piper. Yet as Herman Melville wrote, *the discipline of arms refines*. The military wants the best steel for its officers. Even though the system knows it will never reach a desired level of purity, it's designed to find the dross and pour it off the crucible. The Navy was immune to Peter's charms.

When I finally got ahold of Peter, he pretended the whole affair was overblown. He was determined to fly, be a pilot, and had turned right around and enlisted in the Army Air Force. Even then I marveled at Peter's blind optimism. Only officers got to fly. Didn't he get that? Yet he was sure that his athletic skills would clear the way for an exceptional path to the cockpit. He almost made it. He ended up being the head gunner on a B-29 crew, what they called the central fire control, the crewmember who sits in a chair amidships and directs all attacks against the enemy.

When I say military training brings individual weakness to the fore, I speak from experience. The MIS language school at the Presidio pushed me, all 60 of us in the class, to the limit. I was one of only two non-Japanese in the class. The other was a medical doctor 12 years my senior. He had been a missionary's son in Tokyo and spoke the most beautiful Japanese I'd ever heard – pure poetry – coming from a gaijin's mouth, although I was probably his equal in reading comprehension. I was comforted when he, like me, struggled with the military terms.

After language school, I got shuttled around then shipped to Hawaii. I saw the war through small, ill-lit rooms, hot and humid, as I interrogated high-value Japanese prisoners of war. I worked at a facility located just outside Honolulu called Camp Iroquois, a top-secret camp with a spectacular view of Mamala Bay. I became competent at interrogation because I didn't threaten the captive. I was quiet, orderly, empathetic, and doggedly persistent. For someone who spent seven years in uniform, I confess to no love of the military. Yet I had a feel for what bureaucratic society valued. Plus, I occupied a special niche that few others could fill. The path to indispensability lies in having what your bosses feel they cannot do without.

IX
Bliss

Noriko did not take me home the night after our first date but the sexual tension between us, so palpable, couldn't last long without release.

For the next week or so, however, papers and reports piled upon my desk like it was some sort of repository for military documents. I cringed each time someone knocked on my door. I felt like ripping the phone cord out of the wall. Noriko's editorial position equaled mine for devotion to the office, although she could arrive as late as 10 AM, a luxury I envied. But she was there until sometimes even midnight. We managed to talk on the telephone. I would lie on my bed at night, watching the fan spin on its axis, thinking of nothing but her.

In what free time I had, I began inquiring about the Shibusawa family or Noriko. My initial diggings came up with little other they were from a Choshu clan, historically notable because they helped dispose of the Togukowa shogunate in 1868. That was a long time ago, well, not so long actually, for a nation with a 2600-year-old monarchy.

I asked a Japanese associate at SCAP about the family. He was as opaque as Mrs. Ogawa, but the next day he brought in a book with a section about Noriko's maternal grandfather being a *genrō*, one of the omnipotent counselors who advised the emperor after the Meiji Restoration. These men, at the height of their influence, were among the powerful in Japan.

I tried again to engage Mrs. Ogawa on the topic. The only particular I extracted was that Shibusawa family was very rich but they were not, she hastened to add, *narikin*, which roughly translates to parvenu. But it also meant they made their money within the acceptably sanctioned financial system.

I decided to drop the search for the time being.

Finally, we found time for another date. Noriko and I spent two hours at Mrs. Ogawa's discussing the *wabi* and the *sabi*, or rustic simplicity and grace of Japanese art. Noriko found it interesting but too stilted and hidebound.

"Look at this," she said, opening her purse. She extracted a piece of page from a magazine, folded, with origami precision, into four sections. Noriko carefully opened the worn sheet. It was a page from LIFE magazine of Picasso's Guernica, a piece of work I'd never seen before. Its violent image set me back.

"No Japanese would be able to create a work like this," she said. "That's because we're so worried about offending or working outside our acceptable notions of art. We don't question." She carefully laid the sheet down on the table. "That's what got us into this war."

I was a goner. Any woman, any Japanese woman, moreover, who would carry around such a revolutionary image in her purse, had my utter devotion. I wanted to kiss her right there but knew that would violate Japanese etiquette against public displays of affection, even for this unorthodox woman.

Eventually I said it was late and my agenda the next day was discouragingly full. I paid the bill, used the bathroom, and we left.

Still, I couldn't part without kissing her. During the latter part of our evening, I planned how I would do it. There was a tree just outside the stairwell to Mrs.

Ogawa's. I would steer Noriko to the base of this tree, gently press her against its rough bark and kiss her. It was time. That's all I wanted. Just one kiss.

At the top of the stairs, however, Noriko took my arm – our first contact – and tugged me in the opposite direction as my hotel. I did not resist.

We were the only ones to board a streetcar heading in a northwest direction. I didn't ask our destination. In under ten minutes, we stepped off the trolley at Nippori Station in the Yanaka district, one of the oldest and most traditional parts of Tokyo filled with narrow streets and paths, some unpaved.

At the time, electricity was scarce and expensive. Only the occasional flickering street light or a low-watt bulb coming from an apartment on a second story provided illumination during our walk. A car or a bicycle occasionally drove by and, from a distance, we could hear a streetcar passing, but otherwise our footsteps made the most prominent sound. It had begun to rain very gently, a mist almost but neither of us spoke about the need for an umbrella.

My whole body quivered. I kept telling myself to not project what would happen but the image of us tangled naked in bed could not be denied. We spoke little and shortly Noriko pulled slightly on my arm, guiding me down an alley dark as perdition. When we got to the end, she said, "take a right and up those stairs in front of you."

I could barely make out the steps but Noriko guided us to the first tread. A sliding door, light softly glowing through the rice paper panels, awaited us like a beacon at the top of the stairs. When we reached the landing, the door slid open and a petite woman in the Japanese version of a housecoat stood there. She bowed. We bowed back, although Noriko's bend was more perfunctory than polite.

Who was this?

Noriko had not mentioned she had a roommate. My romantic and steamy projections began to fade. In Japanese, Noriko introduced the woman as "my assistant," which I realized meant, "my maid." Her name was Atsuko. She bowed again, said it was her honor to meet me. She was in her mid-to-late thirties, nondescript, unexceptional in beauty and endowed with a servant's ability to be invisible. We slipped off our shoes and Atsuko knelt down and took them, placing them on a rack against the wall. She then took our coats, first mine, then Noriko's, and hung them in a tiny closet. Then she removed her housecoat, hung it in the closet, took out her own coat and put it on. She bowed again, excused herself, backed out the door, sliding it behind her.

Like the Chiyoda district, much of Yanaka managed to avoid the bombings. It must have been extremely difficult to acquire an apartment there. I myself lived in a hotel because SCAP could find me no housing. How did a single woman, living with a maid manage to acquire such an apartment, when there were thousands of families who were homeless or living in structures cobbled together from material salvaged from destroyed homes?

It was what the Japanese called a three K's: three rooms and a kitchen, a palace at the time.

When I stepped over the threshold, I did more than just enter a coveted apartment; I walked into the home of an *otaku*, a person obsessed with western culture. In Noriko's case, the focus was on impressionist and modern art. I recognized a few of the standbys hanging on the wall – Van Gogh, Picasso, Munch, and Mondrian. In the tiny kitchen, there was a framed covered of a 1940s *Art News* illustrated with a sitting Reuben-esque nude fooling with her hair. No idea the artist. I knew more about Japanese art than western, modern, classical or otherwise. Noriko, it turns out, would teach me. Guernica was just the first lesson.

In the living room stood two bookshelves loaded with books on English and American literature. There were a few concessions to Japanese culture. Yet it was one the only Japanese homes I'd visited that had no *butsudan*, or ancestor shrine. Instead, Noriko's living room had a *tokonoma*, or secular alter, that contained two items: an ancient scroll of Kwan-yin, the Buddhist goddess of mercy, and a heart-haltingly beautiful azul bowl decorated with dolphins, which I later found out came from 15th century Iran.

I could hear water running. I looked at Noriko, a little alarmed that something was spilling over. She waved her hand, unconcerned. "It's just the tap running into the tub. When you were in the loo, I telephoned Atsuko so our bath would be ready for us."

My marveling that she A) had a telephone in her home, very rare and B) had her own soaking tub, usually only found in public baths or in the homes of the wealthy, and C) she had access to enough hot water to fill a tub, was immediately overridden by the fact that Noriko was asking me to get naked with her.

Noriko approached me, reached up and put her arms around my shoulders. One hand pressed the back of my neck. She stood on tiptoe and looked into my eyes. I bent down and we kissed. I could smell her perfume and taste the sweet residue of sake on her tongue. Then she gently pulled back and, for the first time, used the nickname she would hence call me in private: *Noppo,* short for *Seitakanoppo*, or beanpole.

"All day long, Noppo, as I edited manuscripts and argued with my silly bosses over content, I had just one thing in my mind: how much I wanted to wash and scrub that body of yours then get it into my tub."

My tub, might as well have been *my bed*, which I now knew was also on the agenda. This time, I took the initiative and kissed her, deeply.

As we age we forget. But some events do not fade. As I said, I am not a man skilled in the art of seduction. Yet when I kissed Noriko that night, something simultaneously melted and exploded with all the might and light of a supernova. It was more than just lust. I felt my loneliness evaporate and fulfilled my yearning for conversation on topics other than legal or civic issues. I also simply craved human affection.

This was the Japan I was seeking.

We never made it to the tub. Well, we did but only after making a total shambles out of the bed Atsuko had laid out on the tatami. The act of washing each other's bodies, the necessary ritual before getting into any Japanese bath, proved an act so incendiary that the soak had to wait. We were only halfway dried off from our scrub before I picked up her warm, lithe and freckled body and carried her into the bedroom.

Passion burned off the residual water beaded on our skin.

At first I feared Noriko's desire might be a facade orchestrated to attract the attention of a gaijin she found interesting or worse, a kind of distraction.

My worry proved misguided. Noriko seemed as eager as I to spend every spare minute together. She continually startled and delighted me not only with her directness but intellectual curiosity. Noriko was definitely not cut from the same quaint cloth as Cho-Cho-San of Madame Butterfly fame. She was not like the Takeda sisters. I had never met any Japanese woman – or man – quite like her.

Passion remained front and center. She had a limitless devotion for coupling and no patience for prudery and dim imagination. Her bookshelf held a small collection of *shunga*, or classical Japanese erotica illustrations rendered from woodblocks. I'd seen some of this racy material in the rare book collection in Michigan. It both shocked and excited me but it was like a nursery school primer compared to what Noriko's books revealed – ménage a trois, women loving women, women doing it with fish and octopus. She had no qualms about opening up a book to an illustration, holding it up and inquire: "what do you think about this, Noppo?"

Thank Christ she didn't favor replicating the sea creature scenes. Still, I blush at what she taught me.

Even when we returned to her apartment in the wee hours from a bar or movie, she wasted no time making her intentions known. I had to ignore the fact there was a maid trying to sleep in the next room separated by only a paper-thin partition. For a modest Lutheran, this took some doing.

Her only rule was the use of condoms. After the first time we had sex, she looked at me sternly and said: "next time, you bring rubbers. No babies."

Thus, as if passing through a magical door, Noriko lead me to the world I'd read about in books, albeit a modern-day version. For my part, I was over the moon. I lived and breathed Noriko. No previous love came anywhere close in power.

And yet, Noriko was the anti-Japan. She consistently bristled against her country's authoritarian proclivities, including its defining cultural attributes. What I found romantic and charming, she considered provincial and boring. After ignoring numerous requests, she finally took me to a tea ceremony at Hamarikyu Garden, which has been in the ritualistic green tea business since 1704. She went through the motions but was clearly bored. Afterwards, I asked her about what she thought about the ceremony.

"Capital *wagashi*," was all she said, referring to the sweet cookies served with the tea.

She preferred the earthy and pedestrian. When it came to traditional theater, Noriko favored Kabuki over the subtle Noh. Kabuki's common themes and over-the-top drama – and wild make up – left her enthralled. She loved the fight scenes.

I found myself gravitating towards Noh for its reliance on imagination and evoking the powers of the inner world. I also oddly identified with the audience's obligation to read a person's emotions and thoughts from the central actors who wear a mask. It was rather like being at a family reunion with my father's Lutheran relatives.

I think I subconsciously related to Noh because most plays have a *Shite* or protagonist and a *Shitetsure*, a supporting actor of the *Shite*. Following my propensity for leaving the lead role to someone else, Noriko was the *Shite* and I, the *Shitetsure*. It took me a while to develop an appreciation for chanting half singing, half vocalization that passes for dialogue. It sounded a lot like caterwauling at first. Plus, for a tree lover, what's not to like about a play whose common – and only – backdrop is a painting of an ancient pine bending in the wind.

Food was just below sex in a prerogative of pleasures. Noriko endowed me with a love of Japanese cuisine which I never lost. Noriko was a smidge under five feet and weighed roughly 100 pounds. On the dance floor, I could easily sweep her off her feet. Yet she could pack away more tuna and squid into that tiny stomach. Unagi, or freshwater eel, was her favorite. Restaurants that specialized in eel dotted Tokyo; Noriko knew the ones that stayed open late. Many a midnight found us nibbling away on eel grilled over charcoal and served with tangy sauce. Noriko also loved the eel liver served with wasabi and the foot-long deep-fried eel spines, dusted with powdered lime and arriving at the table poking out of a horizontal paper cone tied up with nori.

I also fell to the charms of erratic adventurism. We'd be walking down the street and go by a trolley loading passengers. She'd grab my arm and steer me into the queue.

"Where are we going?"

"I don't know, gaijin, let's find out."

What gifts pleased her the most? Not perfume or stockings but cartons of Lucky Strikes I bought at the PX, Hemingway novels, and Fats Waller recordings I found at an obscure record shop that had managed to escape the bombings.

She also continually challenged me, something odd for a Japanese woman. Once when I complained about the hidebound hierarchy of the Army, she looked at me and declared, "you are such a dreamer, Noppo, such an idealist."

"Why?"

"That's how most Japanese live. Like it's the military. Dawn to dusk. We live in the most hierarchical system in the world. We love hierarchy. That's how the militarists gained a foothold and stayed for the 30 years. You are so lucky to be an American."

"So you don't believe in hierarchy? It hasn't seemed to have hurt your family."

"What has hierarchy done for the women of Japan?" she fumed. "Look at what I have to put up with at work? Some men at NHK can barely stand to be in the same room with me. Even after we lost the war, largely due to people frozen in pecking order where it was impossible to criticize your superior. Men are secretly furious at me for having my position. Again, you are so lucky to be an American."

From the first, I wanted Noriko to marry me. Seeing a window, I asked her: "So, would you like to be an American citizen?"

She took the bait, but only partly and slipped her hand into mine. "That's an intriguing thought, Noppo."

I began to speak but she put her finger to my lips. "I know what you're getting at. Don't rush me," then took away her finger and kissed me with passion.

Noriko had limits, however.

While she happily chatted about the Shibusawa clan of yore and her family's time in England, she did not encourage inquiry about how her family fared the last ten years. She let on that both her parents were alive; she had an older brother and sister, both of whom were married. She showed me their pictures. Her family had numerous houses in Kansai prefecture, in Kyoto and a few around Tokyo, the latter of which were damaged or destroyed during the war. During that time, the family spent their time at a rural estate located in Tottori Prefecture. The house had a complete stable (Noriko said she once was an accomplished rider) and beautiful view of Mount Daisen.

"It's in the middle of nowhere. I will take you there some day so you can see for yourself," she said in an effort to seem transparent.

Some Saturday afternoons or Sundays she would disappear. With time together so precious, I resented these absences. When I asked her about these trips, she said in an apologetic voice that she had gone to visit her parents. When asked if I could meet them, she would say something Dickensian, like "all in good time, Noppo, all in good time."

I had by now deduced that Noriko was likely seen as the family eccentric. She was a loner, too, a young woman with few women friends, an oddity in Japan. Her disregard for convention, inattention to dress, still single at 25, and status as a professional woman were at odds with family expectations. And now she was dating and bedding a gaijin.

X

The Crow

I was alone. I knelt down on a bed of golden Aspen leaves, listening to the scoldings of a scrub jay. My back and knees felt good enough after my nap to tend the bed of aster amellus and chrysanthemums Sylvia and I had planted that spring. As a budding octogenarian, the hard part about gardening is descending to earth, followed by the chore of figuring how to get up. Don't worry about the pain, I thought to myself. Be happy you can live with it. Soon gravity will take you down permanently.

I didn't want to rise unless dictated by necessity. Eventually, nature called. I ignored it for as long as I could then, not wanting Sylvia to come home and find a dark spot on my pants, I staggered to my feet, dusted off my knees, and went in the house. When headed for the bathroom, I noticed that the wicker basket that collects the mail slipping through the slot had a few envelopes. I thought nothing of it. Expecting disappointment, I made myself forget that I had sent Noriko a letter at all. Just ten days had passed. When I picked up the letter, I recognized the handwriting immediately; a spike in blood pressure made my temples and inner ear pulse in tandem.

I retreated to the study, sat down, put the letter on my desk and let it sit there. What if she said no? *I never want to see you again. Keep the damned sword.*

I stared at the one photo of Peter I keep displayed on the wall next to my desk. It's a four by five faded black and white, taken by a newspaper photographer. Peter is standing between my parents, arm around each, in his stained football uniform, face triumphant. The University of Idaho had just blanked Oregon State in the 1938 season opener, 13-0, and Peter's performance as quarterback had been pivotal.

Fumbling around in my desk drawer, I found my letter opener and slit open the envelope.

Noriko had chosen to write on washi paper, made from the mulberry bush. Warm in tone, its unbleached and smooth but with a slight texture. On the upper right-hand side of the stationary, a woodblock illustration: a crow in flight with a grub in its mouth heading towards a nest of small mouths pointing skyward. No tree supporting the nest. That was to be supplied by the reader's imagination.

I stared at the image, putting off getting to the text, musing and marveling and hugely relieved. The Japanese see the crow as the symbol of rejuvenation and purification, not in any spiritual sense, either. Crows cleaned up battlefields. If the piece of paper didn't have a single word upon it, this simple illustration alone would have told me this wasn't a letter of rejection.

My dear Noppo:

You cannot imagine the surprise and pleasure I felt upon receiving your letter. At first, I thought I must be in some sort of dream and soon someone would shake me or the alarm would go off and I would awaken disappointed. Although, truth be told, I don't sleep much anymore. I am up long before the world around me awakes.

So many times I have thought of you and regretted, so deeply, the manner in which we parted. You did not deserve such a thing. What I wanted most of all was a chance to sit down with you and explain what happened. I have imagined this scenario – you and I talking, each holding our wrinkled and crooked hands – a hundred times. I have thought about writing yet thoughts scribbled by pen could not adequately carry my feelings. Nor would words spoken over a telephone.

Thus I will not begin my explanations now. However, I would be overjoyed to have one last meeting with you. But I feel it is really too much to ask; it would be such a long journey. Are you able to undertake such a task?

Just let me say now the sword is secondary. Keep it if you wish, although my family would welcome its return. It is up to you. It is a small price for how I mistreated you. I look forward to hearing from you.

With deepest affection,

Noriko

I read the letter again, then set it on my desk, feeling OK but as if I had just emerged from a volcano-hot bath, relieved to escape the heat yet basking from the water's salubrious effects. Noriko's remorseful tone left my slack-jawed in wonder. Genuine contrition did not come easily for her. I didn't quite believe that part about her not wanting the sword.

I was overcome not by panic or fright but by a wave of *mono no aware*, which has no true English translation, really, although it's something like being aware of the impermanence of life, of our intransigent trajectory through this existence. Half a century had passed since I last seen fresh ink from Noriko's pen. It had gone by with the speed of a shooting star. A passage from *the Heike Monogatari* flashed through my mind:

The sound of the Gion shōja bells echoes the impermanence of all things...
The proud do not endure, they are like a dream on a spring night.

I've often thought the closest western pathos of this passage came from John Donne –a favorite of Noriko's – when he wrote *never send to know for whom the bell tolls, it tolls for thee*.

The second thought was less celestial: My God. Unless I croak tomorrow, this is really going to happen. Better have a come-to-Jesus talk with Sylvia. While I put stock in the opinion that discretion is the better part of valor, if my relationship with Noriko confirmed anything, it was that I'm not comfortable with subterfuge and secrets. We all keep goblins in closets but I'd seen relationships that operated daily on confidences. Just being around the participants in such a drama put holes in my stomach.

Sylvia would understand my dilemma, of this I was sure (well, pretty sure), although the sympathy might take time in unfolding.

When she was an undergraduate at the University of Sao Paulo, Sylvia became a professor's mistress, a man 25 years her senior, married and from a notable family. Father of three children. The relationship lasted even after she graduated. It all came tumbling down after she got pregnant. Her Catholic conscience forbade an abortion. She spent a lonely year living with an aunt and uncle in Rio, doing "research," had the baby, and put it up for adoption. She said the day she received her acceptance from the law school at Edinburgh was one of the great moments in her life. She could flee her sorrow of having to give up a child to a new life, although she eventually returned to Brazil.

I knew none of this until after we married. One evening attending a cocktail party at the Sao Paulo house of a stupendously rich Japanese coffee baron, drinking caipirinas and listening to Miles Davis's *Round About Midnight*, Sylvia suddenly grabbed her stomach and collapsed into a chair. The miscarriage triggered a torrent of grief and guilt. Lying with me on a hospital bed, shaking as if she had the palsy, and clutching me so hard it left bruises on my arm, Sylvia wailed she was sure this miscarriage was punishment for being a man's whore, having his child and giving it away.

And my, how the ghosts of the past linger.

About 15 years ago when we were still living in Santa Monica, I came home from work to find my bride tossing letter after letter into a blazing fireplace. It was July, the temperature in the low 90s. A steady stream of tears colored by mascara dripped from Sylvia's face, staining her blouse in a galaxy of dark dots. She was breathing in slow, short gasps. I stood there, not knowing what to say somehow having the sense not to ask or to interrupt. In fact, I wanted to leave as I felt I was a voyeur to an act of contrition. But I didn't move. Sylvia looked at me – a stare of pure sorrow – licked the dark tears from her top lip, bringing them into her mouth, wiped her nose with the back of her hand, then turned away and returned to her task of incineration.

It was a funereal ritual; she wasn't tossing in the letters in one clump. It was one by one, as if each missive required a separate commitment to flame. When she hurled the last envelope in to the flames, I took my handkerchief and handed it to her. She dabbed her eyes, blew her nose with an unfeminine honk, then, looking at the black streaks on it, tossed that too into the fire. Then she came to me, flung her arms around me and buried her head into my chest, a full-on sob.

Finally she said that day she had received a letter from a friend in Sao Paulo that included the obituary of her former lover and father of the child she gave away. The letter triggered a wave of remorse and she remembered the letters, the hundreds of letters, she and this man had written and she saved in the bottom of a sweater chest.

The correspondence had stopped decades ago, she said, but for some reason she saved it all. "Why would I do that, Teddy?" said asked, over and over.

The only real person is a flawed person. I made no attempt to answer, although some of those letters came when we were still married. I think they have something to do with those two children she lost in Brazil. Sometimes when I hear her fussing over Diego in the laundry room, brushing him and crooning, I wonder if she's giving affection to those ghosts.

Then an acceleration of events, arranged by the fates, I suppose.

The day after I received Noriko's letter, we were scheduled to go to Adrian and Melanie's for dinner. We decided, rather spur of the moment, that before we went to their house, we would go for an afternoon hike in the Coconino National Forest for one last look at the foliage. Sylvia drove. We were on an isolated stretch of Lake Mary Road listening to a CD of Benny Goodman's 1938 concert at Carnegie Hall, when a state trooper's Crown Victoria, siren's wailing and lights flashing, roared passed, tires hissing on dry pavement.

Then came an ambulance in a similar state of alarm. We shortly arrived at the cause of their urgency. Pieces of bumper, a taillight sprouting wires, a bent hub cab, half a ski rack, a pillow, patches of sparkling glass, and, most wretchedly, a child's car seat, littered the road. A deputy sheriff in an orange vest hastily kicked the detritus off the road and set out orange cones to nudge drivers to the shoulder. We passed a section of guardrail, bent and uprooted by impact. The vehicle had apparently ricocheted off the guardrail and ended up on a bank on the other side of the road. It was some sort of sleek four-wheel drive and had either gone end-over-end or flipped and rolled extensively. It sat on its roof, which was crookedly crushed by the impact. We could see the vague shape of a body on the driver's side, an arm flopped out the window.

Like I have done my whole life when I see unpleasant things, I averted my eyes forward to the road.

"Oh Dio," said Sylvia as we passed the wreck. "Oh Dio. Why? Why? Why?" she said, asking an existential question although she wasn't expecting me to answer. "Tell me they won't find a child's body in that car or tossed out in the road. Tell me that!"

Just as I could not offer a reason why she kept all those letters from a former lover, I could not, of course, give her assurance that the rescuers would not find a child with a snapped neck.

Sylvia glanced at me and asked with the vehemence of lawyerly inquiry. "Where was the other car, Ted? Tell me that? How did a single vehicle manage to get itself in such a horrible wreck? Look," she motioned to the blue sky though the windshield, like an evangelist pointing towards a cross, her hand shaking: "No rain. No snow. We're on a straightaway for fuck's sake."

I said nothing, just listened to Gene Krupa thump the drums during *Sing, Sing, Sing*.

Diego, picking up on Sylvia's angst, stuck his head between our seats. We both simultaneously began stroking his head like a talisman, comforting both him and ourselves.

"Oh, this unpredictable world!" Sylvia said in a half-sob, wiped her eyes with the back of her hand, and grabbed my fingers over the top of Diego's head.

We drove in silence as we observed another manifestation of the world's mercurial temperament. A storm cloud, almost dark and billowing as a July monsoon – so rare in late October – appeared in the horizon to the south. I had checked the weather that morning. It augured a fine day with a five percent chance of precipitation.

"What's this?" asked Sylvia, turning down the music.

"Wasn't in forecast," I said, mildly defensively.

"Neither was that accident," said Sylvia.

We decided to push on. The closer we got to the trailhead, darker the cloud. It began to rain, then hail, covering the road in an ice layer texture of macadam. The hail alternatively bounced or flatten against the windshield, freezing in place.

"Well, there goes our outing," said Sylvia. "Let's look for a place to turn around."

Wipers on full swipe mode, Sylvia eased off the accelerator and turned the heat defrost full blast. She gently pumped the breaks to test the road conditions. The Camry did a modest and unthreatening shudder then did a complete 360 on the road before coming to a stop on the other lane, all the while Sylvia swearing in Portuguese. I couldn't quite make it out but it had something to do with accusing the Virgin Mary of having carnal acts with residents of the ape house.

But then Sylvia, ever the calm eye in the middle of a hurricane, gunned engine, tires spinning and pointed the car over to our side of the road. She drove over the shoulder and parked under a Ponderosa pine and turned off the engine. Protected by a canopy of needles, the drumming on the roof and assault on the windshield abated enough that we could hear ourselves talk. We both looked at each other, breathing heavily, and both gave grateful grins.

"Whew. My heart," she said, clutching her chest, "barely survived that one. Plus I have a strict rule on tragedies," she said, holding up her shaking right index finger. "One per day is my limit," she said looking at me with relief and a sigh. She grabbed my hand then beckoned Diego out of the back seat. He happily obliged and, after some adjustment, arranged all sixty pounds of himself on Sylvia's lap. She hugged him like a child might hug a teddy bear and rolled down the window the width of a dog's nose.

I forget which callous wit remarked that nature is hanging a judge. If a car or truck had been travelling in the other lane, we could have ended up worse than that twisted SUV. Seems shallow but instead of thinking about how I would miss Sylvia or my grandchildren, I remained fixated how I would have been denied my quest to settle accounts with Noriko. Thus, out of the blue, I blurted:

"I found the owner of the sword in Japan."

Sylvia glanced over at me, puzzled. "What?"

Then she put together the timing of the statement. "Nothing like the *sombra da morte* to hasten obligations, eh Teddy?" she said, smiling slightly.

"Yes. That's right. That's exactly right, Sylvia."

"So using that computer program or service or whatever it's called paid off?"

"Yes."

"Then what did you do? Tell me."

"I wrote her."

"Her. Noriko?"

"Sent the letter by FedEx."

"Uh-huh. And?"

"She wrote me back."

"When did this happen?" she said, unable or unwilling to control a slight waver of anxiety in her voice.

"The letter arrived yesterday," I said, and waited for Sylvia to start muttering in her native tongue, "I'll show it to you when we get home."

She was silent, looked out the crack in the foggy window, then said, "Well," in a tone that told me my honesty and openness had thwarted an assault. "What did she say?"

I forced myself not to eliminate what Sylvia might not want to hear. "She apologized for ending the relationship the way she did – cutting me off with no explanation and refusing all further contact. She said she would welcome a chance to explain what happened, face-to-face conversation preferred."

"Well, I can understand that," said Sylvia, in a detached voice. "And the sword?"

"It's up to me. She considered the theft of the sword payment for how she treated me."

"My. That's rather dramatic," said Sylvia. "Contrition bordering on martyrdom. And what do you think?"

"About the returning the sword? Like I said last week, I've kept it way too long. It needs to be returned from whence in came. That's to Noriko or someone in her family. Now that I have her address, I could mail it. But I think it's best if I do it in person."

"That's a long way to go for person who doesn't like flying for more than four hours at a stretch," she said. "Think of your back. Can't you mail it?"

"Nick said I can but I don't think that would address the issue."

"What is the issue, Teddy?"

"I think, Sylvia, I think it's the dream that I want to die unencumbered. Beholden to no one. I can't do that if I mail the sword. I'll fly to Hawaii to Osaka. Rest a day, then on to Tokyo."

"Do you want me to come?"

I knew she'd ask this question.

"I think I best do this journey alone."

Sylvia was silent. Too silent.

"Are you jealous, Sylvia? Noriko's now 79 years old and three grown children. Hardly a candidate for extra marital exploration."

She sighed again, buried her face in Diego's fur, then said, "I know, *meu amor*. It's just that old romances can have almost an unnatural power over us for the rest of our lives. You know I speak from experience. We yearn for what might have been. We imagine happiness and bliss even though deep down inside we know there are good reasons why the relationship fell apart. Still, sometimes when our present lives seem wearisome and nothing but struggle, that yearning can take over. Be careful, Teddy."

Scottish sensibility pulled through. I relaxed a bit.

"There's something else, Sylvia."

"What's that?" she asked a little warily, moving Diego around on her lap.

"The sword," I began carefully, checking my words, looking out the side window. "The sword represents something besides love gone bad. It somehow connects with how Peter died."

Sylvia looked at me, not expecting this reply. She nodded very slightly, curious but respectful.

"What? Really? How he died at the hands of the Japanese?" she asked.

"Yes," I said, "something like that," turning back to the window and the sleet outside. My lips had gone dry. "I'm not very good at talking about it. Sorry. I spoke to Alice about it and even that was a pretty short conversation. She said she didn't have the constitution to hear about the horrible details. But just broaching the subject helped."

I could feel the lump of rage rising in my throat. I continued.

"Alice said I needed to talk about it with other men, men my age. I tried to talk to Walt about it. You know, the guy I see around Bushmaster Park. You know he's former military and had a brother in Singapore. Waste of effort. Wasn't remotely sympathetic. So, I'm somehow hoping this trip to Japan, traveling with the sword, will help me come to terms with my outrage."

I turned to look at Sylvia. Both she and Diego were looking straight at me.

"I think that's all I can say right now."

Sylvia reached over and gently messaged the back of neck. "That's all right, *meu amor*, you've said quite enough."

When she touched me, I could feel the lump in my throat begin to subside.

The next night, Sylvia made a dish using cannellini beans and what she calls *acelga vermelha*, a type of red chard favored in Brazilian cooking. We both like the vegetable for its range of flavors, which can go from almost acrid to buttery sweet. She watched me eat, appreciating that I had at least a modest appetite. "Best to blend bitter and sweet on the same fork, eh Teddy?"

XI

Open window

Half asleep, I heard Atsuko rustling around in the kitchen, heating water for our tea. Shortly she would enter the bedroom with a lacquered tray holding two cups and a pot of green tea. She would kneel, bow, set the tray by the bed, bow again, and then leave, sliding the door behind her.

When the tea arrived, Noriko stirred then pushed herself up. Usually, she poured promptly because she did not favor strong tea. On that morning, however, she ignored the teapot and shoved aside the bedcovers, rolled out of bed, devoid of any pajamas or nighty, and went to the window, peaking outside. "Ah," she said in obvious delight, bouncing a little on the balls of her feet, "it is just as the weatherman promised. A splendid day! The first really nice day of spring."

She came back to bed, momentarily straddled me over the futon, and bent down and kissed me.

"I have a surprise for you."

"Oh?"

"Yes, indeed." Then she rolled off and attended to the business of pouring the tea. I put on my glasses and sat up in bed, not so much wondering about the surprise as reveling in the lovely sight of a naked pale woman making tea, and doing so without a flicker of self-consciousness.

"Well?" I asked.

She held up her finger that I should wait.

When we both had our cups on hand and Noriko had tucked herself back under the covers. Noriko blew across her cup to cool the tea. "We're going to meet my family."

I almost spilled the contents of my handle-less cup. I had been waiting for this day for months. "You don't say? Where?"

"Rikugien Garden. It's in the northern part of the city that was mostly spared damage from the war. It's in the Bunkyo ward. Have you ever been there?"

I had not. But I was excited and curious. This was a big deal and one that offered affirmation that Noriko was serious about getting married.

"Who will be there today?"

Noriko took another sip of her tea. "My father and brother for sure. My mother. My sister cannot attend."

"How long has this outing been in the works?"

"Oh, awhile. My brother in particular wants to meet you. I think you'll like him."

"And your parents? Will they like me?"

"Oh Noppo. Don't ask me such a question. They will be polite and formal. My father's English is excellent as is my brother's. They are curious about you. But you are still gaijin, yes? So…" she shrugged her shoulders as if to say I shouldn't expect too much.

"And your mother?"

"Her English is fairly rudimentary, although she understands more than she lets on. Quite a bit, actually. She will mostly remain quiet, however, and let the men do the talking. Do not expect a direct conversation. In some ways, she doesn't reside in this world. She lost her two brothers and three nephews in the war. She's spends a good deal of the day communing with them. She believes that the spirits of the dead guide the living."

She put her index finger on my arm and pressed hard enough into my flesh make an indentation. "Wear your best suit."

It was an odd but illuminating meeting from the start. I assumed, after returning home and donning my suit, that I would meet Noriko and we would take the trolley to Rikugien Garden. That was the first of a series of naïve conclusions about that day. I was to go there alone.

It was the start of cherry blossom season; Rikugien Garden was packed with visitors hoping for a glimpse of an early blossom. It was indeed a warm spring day. During the walk from the station to the gardens, I worked up a sweat in my light wool jacket but decided to leave it on. I was about to undergo an inspection. I didn't want to admit to myself how badly I sought approval. As luck would have it, I just had my suit cleaned and comforted myself that I looked halfway presentable.

We were to meet at a spot in the garden called the Tsutsuji-no-chaya teahouse, a thatched rustic open-walled affair in the garden built in the Meiji period. Visitors favored it mostly during the fall to gape at the foliage. Noriko thought that it being spring, it might be less crowded.

It was, but density is a subjective term. In Pocatello they would have called this a mob. There were a lot of people milling around the teahouse, jockeying for the few available seats. But Noriko was right. There were fewer folks than in the cherry tree section of the park. Knowing the Japanese penchant for punctuality, I was a few minutes early. I looked around and saw no one I recognized. The humming birds and bees provided a constant background buzz.

I felt the familiar discomfort of being an object of attention. No matter where I went in Japan, my height and blonde hair, even cut short as it was, drew stares. It was worse when I was forced to remain stationary, such as tanding at a streetcar stop. In my presence, the Japanese forgot their normal etiquette of avoiding behavior that would make people uncomfortable. The day before, when standing in a line at a shop, an elderly couple had actually put down their shopping bags so they could indulge in a closer inspection. The introvert in me squirmed.

I noticed a man walking towards me. He was slim, a little over five feet tall and about 30. Raven hair studiously uncoiffed capped an aristocratic and alert face. An immaculately tailored light gray suit, probably stitched in Milan or Seville Row, draped over his slight frame almost too perfectly. Underneath, a white starched shirt gleamed, accented by a dark silk tie. His shined shoes clacked on the stone as he approached.

He stopped in front of me and bowed.

"Theodore Lundquist?" he asked.

"Yes," I said and instinctively gave a polite bow in return.

The man gave a shallow bob of the head in return and gave a polite laugh, "Ah, I jolly well thought it had to be you," he said, with only the slightest accent. "You're hard to miss, you and your height. I'll bet you get tired of all the staring, what?"

He held out his hand. "Takakichi Shibusawa," he said, "Pleasure to make your acquaintance. Please just call me Taki. Everyone else does, including my parents."

We gave a brief shake, Taki's hand warm, lithe, and soft as a child's. Then he gave a slight gesture with his left hand towards one of the benches. At one end sat an older man, what hair was left on his head gray, wearing round turtle-shell glasses, also dressed in a beautiful suit. Two women wearing kimonos sat beside him. The two women, however, sat facing the other way with their backs turned to the inside of the teahouse. They were gazing down the hill at the spring foliage, their heads bobbed subtlety in conversation. So, I thought, Noriko's sister must have come after all.

Meanwhile, I was searching the area for Noriko. Where the hell was she?

The older gentlemen rose a little stiffly, bowing, smiling warmly at me, saying something to the two women. They, too, rose and turned. I caught my breath.

Noriko wore a stunning peach-colored *furisode* kimono – the baggy sleeved variety favored by unmarried women – the silk shot through with pale green leaves. A patina of powder covered her freckles. Her hair was pulled up in the classical style. Mrs. Shibusawa was decked out in a *kuro tomesode*, a formal kimono I'd only seen worn by wives at high-end diplomatic functions. Black, with gold phoenixes cascading below the waist, a series of family crests, also in gold, rested on the kimono's shoulders and arms. She must be absolutely roasting, I thought. And yet I was flattered and took her choice of dress as an auspicious sign: a *kuro tomesode* is a garment of welcome.

Noriko looked at me for a millisecond, gave the briefest flicker of a smile, lowered her eyes then joined her mother and father in giving me a bow. The older of the two women looked as if she was doing her best not to show weariness and exhaustion.

Formality, Noriko had forewarned, would preside during this introduction. "Do not try and shake my mother's hand. Just bow and stare at her outrageously expensive *zori* (the obligatory footwear for kimonos). No gifts, either. That would create an unpleasant obligation. And do not, my darling Noppo, make any attempt to hold my hand, not even rub knuckles. Such behavior will make my parents uncomfortable."

It chapped me a bit to have Noriko lecture me on this protocol like I was some newcomer to Japan. The evenings spent as an interpreter with the diplomatic section had schooled me in Nipponese social niceties. I was curious why Noriko felt obliged to bring them up. Later – why is it always later? – I saw this as the first sign that in spite of Noriko's iconoclastic behavior, she had ironclad fealty to the culture of kin.

Or maybe it was because Noriko could see through my flimsy confidence. On the streetcar to Rikugien, I nervously rehearsed my behavior: speak softly, use the sentence structure of respect, be humble, don't blow my nose into my handkerchief, don't stand around my hands in my pockets, no public displays of affection, of course, and, above all, no questions about the war.

Still, I was not expecting this level of rigidity.

Mr. Shibusawa spoke the kind of English I'd only heard in conversations with the occasional visiting professor at Michigan or the high-ranking officers of the British occupation force. It wasn't the nasally, sharp-vowelled bark of the Australians or New Zealanders, but the mellifluous tongue native to that green and pleasant land. They had attended Cambridge or Sandhurst and were full of smooth, facile, and understated phrases. Like his son, Mr. Shibusawa had only the slightest trace of a Japanese accent.

The senior Shibusawa suggested we go for stroll. The men walked up front while Noriko and her mother followed ten paces behind. Although I had seen this segregated arrangement plenty of times, it felt odd and alienating to be a participant. I had to force myself to keep walking with Taki and Mr. Shibusawa; I wanted to wait for Noriko and her mother to catch up. I kept wondering how Noriko was doing. Why didn't she warn me of this?

A polite and predictable conversation followed. Taki served as the ringmaster. We even spoke in Japanese for a few minutes. He was effusively complementary about my grasp of his native tongue and fawned over the fact I had gone to the University of Michigan, which he asserted was one of the leading public institutions in America.

He wanted to know: What exactly did I do at SCAP? Where was I residing? How did I like Japan? When did I plan to return to America?

These were unusual direct queries, confirming my suspicious I would be put to some sort of cultural test. Taki was also obliging me to talk excessively about myself, a faux pas in Japan. Was I able to shut my mouth? Yet asking them questions presented landmines. They were an old rich family who had probably evaded much of the suffering Japan had gone through the last ten years. What were they going to say?

I delicately inquired about their ancestors who helped restore the emperor. They gave replies of modesty, saying that scholars had probably over estimated their family's role in history. They became slightly more engaged when I ask Mr. Shibusawa about his time in England. He spoke at length about his admiration for the British, particularly the fairness of the legal system. As we passed over the garden's famed Togetsukyo Bridge, Mr. Shibusawa, stopped and looked down at the water.

"In many ways, the United Kingdom and Japan are alike," he summed up. "Two island nations who became powerful despite their size and isolation. We both have traditions that have carried through the centuries. But, unfortunately," he paused, "Japan has made some regrettable choices as of late, ones that never would have been made in Whitehall."

The only time the conversation relaxed and become remotely authentic was when Mr. Shibusawa inquired about my father. He asked, ever so genteelly, "how does your father occupy his time?"

When I said he was an assistant professor of horticulture, the two men could not hide their pleasure, heads nodding like articulated wooden penguins with approval. Mr. Shibusawa asserted that surely there was not a more honorable and interesting profession than studying plants and flowers. Somehow, I felt as if my father's occupation, acquired through thousands of hours of menial extension work, had bestowed upon me a form of aristocratic approval.

We made one glacial lap around the lake before Taki announced that his mother was probably tired and he must attend to her needs. I was mindful to give a low and long bow to the parents and to Taki, back straight, past 30 degrees almost looking directly at my shoes, which, in contrast to every pair worn by the Shibusawa clan, were large, worn, and clumsily polished. Noriko left with them. She had never said a word.

###

Had I passed inspection or merited any sort of approval? I flattered myself I did, but, to my exasperation, Noriko clammed up when it came to discussing her family's opinion of me, besides that they enjoyed my company and were impressed by my Japanese. Her clipped reply should have set off warning bells but when you're in head-over-heels, you never hear the clapper hit the steel dome of doom.

Moreover, Noriko's behavior at Rikugien threw me for a loop. She had barely acknowledged me and reverted to a shy, fealty-bound maiden. Worry continued to build until, needing some certainty and assurance, on a pleasant spring evening, I asked Noriko to marry me. I even had a ring, a real beauty with diamonds and lapis I bought from a pawnshop that was run the Yakuza. We had explored the idea of marriage numerous times and, in my mind, she embraced the idea. It was understood that after I was done with my duties at SCAP, we would wed and move to California.

I was shocked and disappointed when she said she was honored and the ring was lovely, but she had to think about it a little more. I wanted to yell: "what is there to think about?"

But I didn't yell. I dug a hole in my psyche and buried my anger and hurt. A week later, my commanding officer pulled me aside. He told me my diligence and long hours had not gone unnoticed. Wasn't it time for some R&R?

Pan American Airways, flying their Boeing 377 Stratocruiser, was planning a direct flight from Tokyo to Hawaii. Before officially announcing this development, Pan American embarked on a series of test runs and entered into a short-term contract with the military to freight personnel from Tokyo to Honolulu and return. My boss asked: "We could make a seat available to you…and your girl. Right now they're doing two flights a week, both to and from Hono. Interested?"

The offer was a deep compliment. My boss knew of my relationship with Noriko, officially forbidden. Not only had he looked the other way, but was sanctioning a trip for both of us on the military's dime.

The thought of escaping Tokyo's dank spring and seeing Noriko prancing around on the sand in the latest rage in beachwear, the bikini (something I knew she wouldn't hesitate to wear), put me in a swoon. I welcomed a respite from work. I dreamt about grilled cheese sandwiches and hankered to hear English on the streets and stop being gawked at like a freak.

Arranging the trip to Hawaii took some doing. Noriko ricocheted between enthusiasm and worry. The idea of the trip thrilled her, but said she was worried about her job, which seemed plausible at first. She held an important place at NHK, the only woman to have gained a managerial position. Women executives were extremely rare; Noriko told me she was one of the highest-paid businesswomen in Japan and that she had fought for every yen she earned, although was that was a bit dramatic.

She had gotten the job at the very end of the war. NHK realized they had some serious accommodation ahead of them when it came understanding the pathos of the English language. But, no matter. Noriko was an exception as the Japanese promote on tenure and age, not so much talent. Although her extraordinary English language and writing skills – not to mention family background – gave her job safety, a ten-day absence concerned her. This was not a time when Japanese favored vacations; they looked down on those who did.

I became so concerned that I, without consultation from Noriko, dressed in a freshly pressed captain's uniform and paid a personal call to the president of NHK. The uniform was important because it showed my rank. This would set the chairman, a former military man, at ease.

He knew where we stood in our respective hierarchies. I guessed he would see us as equals, with perhaps him elevated slightly, all the better, because it gave me the opportunity to employ a humility and an appreciation for superiors. He assured me Noriko's status at the company would not suffer if she took time off.

Not only did Noriko continue to waffle on her decision to come, but she began avoiding me.

My commanding officer told me one morning he needed a decision about the trip. I left the office and took the trolley straight to her apartment. It was still early enough I could catch her at home. I was about to knock on her door when heard shouts of anger from within. I thought Noriko was giving Atsuko a hiding but I'd never heard Noriko ever use that tone of voice with her. I had never heard Noriko use that voice, ever.

When I overheard the words *Hawaii* and *giri* (obligation), I realized she was on the telephone and our trip was the topic of the call. The speaker on the other end did not approve. As oddly individualistic and autonomous as she was, I could not imagine Noriko speaking like that to her formal parents, especially when I heard the phrase *shinjimae*, which means go to hell, said not once, but twice.

Then she shrieked, employing her excellent command of the English obscenity: *fuck-off* and slammed down the receiver. There was a pause and something breakable got swatted off a table or thrown as there was sound of smashing. I wanted to turn and head right back down the stairs but this trip to Hawaii was on the line. I knocked.

I expected Atsuko to open the door but it was her boss instead. Noriko wore a disheveled mustard-colored dressing gown of raw silk. Her freckles stood out like pimples against a face pale as plaster; her hair looked as if it has been subject to hurricane forces. Red welts from crying circled her eyes.

She pulled her head back, shocked to see me and barked: "Gaijin! What are you doing here?"

I said nothing but backed away from the door. But before I could get out of arm's length, she reached out and grabbed me by the sleeve of my uniform. "Oh, Noppo, that you should see me like this. I am so ashamed." She hung her head and her shoulders began to shake. I had heard Noriko moan and shout and spit tears in the heat of passion, but I had never seen her in such a state.

She looked up and took my hand. "Please. Come in. Forgive the mess. Atsuko has gone to visit her parents."

Noriko led me into the kitchen, passing the bedroom along the way. Her futon had not been put away. Clothes littered the floor. In the kitchen, unwashed cups, bento boxes, and bowls covered the counter and table. I had never seen such disarray in a Japan home. She cleared a spot on the tiny kitchen table and pulled out a chair.

"Please sit," she said, and kissed me briefly on the mouth before I sat. Her mouth tasted of stale tea and sake.

"Thank you," she said.

"Thank you for what? I asked.

"For kissing me. I don't feel I am worthy of a kiss right now."

"That's silly," I protested and kissed her again.

She allowed the second kiss then turned her head away. "No, not so silly. Oh, Noppo," and said again, "that you should see me and this house like this."

"What's going on, baby? Who was that on the telephone?"

"I will explain. But let me heat water for tea first."

She lit the stove, put on the kettle, then began to search for a pair of clean cups. "Your invitation to Hawaii has created a disturbance in the house of Shibusawa," she said, her voice flat. "It has pitted my brother and my mother against my father. Everything is upside down."

"Please explain."

"Only on the condition that you forgive my direct way of speaking."

"But Noriko, you've always been straightforward with me. That's one of the things I love about you."

She smiled weakly, lips tight. "Sometimes. Other times, I'm very Japanese. I can say no in a thousand ways without ever saying the word."

She sat down and took a Lucky Strike out of a nearly empty pack; it sat next to an overflowing ashtray. I saw the box of matches before she did and lit her cigarette. She nodded in appreciation and brushed her hair out of her eyes. She looked around the room, trying to choose her words. Finally she said:

"This is not my father's fault, just to let you know. All foreigners tend to think a romance with a Japanese woman runs into trouble because her father forbids it. But my father likes you very much, Noppo. He thinks we ought to get married. In any other Japanese household, that would be the end of the story. But I will confess that my father is a weak man with no stomach for confrontation. No lord of the manor, he. It's my mother. I have been one disappointment after another for her. My relationship with you is yet another blow. In her mind, our relationship is something she must endure but not accept. She comforts herself it will end soon or, at the very longest, when you leave Japan. This trip to Hawaii frightens her very much."

"That was your mother you were talking to?" I couldn't believe that.

She smiled at my naiveté then shook her head. "Oh, no, Noppo. That was Taki. I have mentioned before that my mother and Taki are very close. Well, here's an example. He was doing her speaking for her."

"I see."

She sighed and almost whispered, "so complicated."

"As you know, Noppo, we come from a very old family, my mother's clan in particular, an imperial line. Her father served the Emperor Meiji. She really believes the Japanese are a divine race."

This could mean nothing good for me. I answered in Japanese. *Sou desu ne*. Uh-huh.

Noriko nodded but watched the tip of her cigarette burn. It was so still that the smoke drifted up in a straight line and curled against the ceiling. "In her opinion, to wield a sword to defend the clan or family name is honorable. To take up a gun to defend a nation is not. In other words, she subscribes to an ancient belief that the military is a base calling. There's no little contradiction here because her family is riddled with military men. Still, the thought that I might marry a man committed to the military threatens her."

Military man? I began to protest. Noriko silenced me a somber glance.

"I know, Noppo, I know. The army is only temporary for you. Deep down inside you are a scholar. My father understands that. My mother does not. Taki understands, I think, but he has obligations to my mother. Furthermore Taki, like my father, respects you, but he thinks you are – how does one say this? – rough around the edges. He thinks I can do better. Plus, Noppo, there is something I cannot really explain and I take no pleasure in trying. I know I've been evasive on what my family did during the war. Well, I will tell you now, although you've probably figured it out: my father hid away on his estates and let Taki run company affairs. I, like my father, buried my head in the sand reading Shakespeare and Keats. I read and re-read my father's *Oxford Book of English Verse.* Secluded. I would spend day upon day listening to Basil Rathbone read a Christmas Carol. I made it my business not to inquire about my family's commercial affairs. Taki oversaw all that and we never spoke about it."

I found this hard to believe. "Never?"

She sighed deeply. "You Americans are sometimes so blind to our helplessness. We are powerless to the whims of fate. Sometimes Taki would have big shots from the military visit our home in Kyoto. My parents, because they were loyal Japanese, tolerated this, although they both despised the militarists, my mother in particular hated it, although she liked the order they created. My presence was required at some of these affairs but my role was to be the quiet and submissive daughter. I was never included in any serious conversation besides, there was an ironclad protocol that business was not something you discussed at our household dinner. Too vulgar. So, no, I never knew what Shibusawa Trading, Ltd, did during the war. But…"

She paused, started to talk again, then stopped. My interrogator's instinct said she was hiding something, something fairly important.

I reached out and took her free hand. "But, what, Noriko?"

She shook her head and kissed the back of my hand. "I am so much trouble. So sorry Noppo."

The kettle began to boil. She crushed her half-smoked cigarette and rose to turn off the burner. Instead of arranging the tea, she went to the bathroom. I could hear faint tinkling and splashing sounds. When she emerged from the bathroom, her robe hung open. It opened further as she walked towards me. There was nothing underneath. She stopped in front of me. Filled with wonder as I always was at the sight of her nakedness, I also felt apprehension. Noriko was almost always the initiator, but not like this. Usually she would start by fiddling and pawing at my clothes. Sometimes, when the heat was unusually high and I wasn't reciprocating fast enough in taking off her garment, she'd start ripping off her own clothes.

Now, she stood in front of me, emanating a passivity and I could not help but be aroused. She put her hand under my chin and made me look at her, her eyes searching mine.

I did not bother to untie my shoes nor take off my socks. It was short and furious and we did not even think about using a condom.

Afterward, as we lay there, Noriko said, "Noppo, if you want me to come to Hawaii, then you must tell me I have to come."

"Sorry?"

"You are asking me to make a choice, a very difficult choice. My mother and Taki do not want me to go. You do, very much, I feel. Am I wrong?"

"Absolutely I want you to come, but not at gunpoint. That choice is yours."

"It's too big a choice for me. Please. Tell me I must come to Hawaii and I will go with you."

"Well, OK," I said, going along. Commands outside the military and the Yakuza are considered rude. "Noriko, please come to Hawaii with me."

She propped herself up on one elbow and looked at me. "No, Noppo. Do not include a single syllable of equivocation or choice or any nicety. This is not a request. It is an order. A command. *Meirei*," she said, the word for imperative.

She looked at me ruefully. "Are you capable of that?"

"And if I'm not?"

"Then," she said, sweeping her hand about her disheveled room. "You leave me in this mess."

To be responsible not only for Noriko declining a trip to Honolulu but leaving her in a state of anarchic limbo tipped the scales of my Lutheran guilt. Still, I hesitated. "What of the situation with your family?"

"My family," she said gravely, "has survived many more severe forms of submission, Noppo. Do not worry about that. It will work out. Just you wait and see."

On that optimistic note, I said: "Noriko. We leave for Honolulu in eleven days. Have your work arrangements completed. I need your passport by tomorrow so I can arrange for a special permit. Understood?"

She bowed her tangled head of hair so far I could see her freckled neck. "*Hai*," she said.

Again, why is it always later? Why didn't I understand until months afterwards that the shocking state of Noriko's apartment wasn't the result of her being upset about a family feud? It was because Noriko's wealth and status prevented her from taking responsibility for her messes. That was for a servant to clean up.

The trip to Hawaii provided another lesson I did not want to heed. The venture was mostly glorious. But the last day we had a quarrel in our hotel room. It was brief but left scars.

She sat on the bed, looking out the window at the beach, pensively staring at the waves.

"What's wrong, baby?"

Noriko continued to look out the window.

"You feeling OK?"

"Oh, Noppo. I don't know."

"Don't know what?"

"I don't know about living in America. I saw the way some people looked at me in here, especially the clerk of this hotel. Contempt if not outright hate. And that cab driver who pretended I wasn't even there and talked about his experiences fighting the Japs."

She turned and looked at me. "Why didn't you say something, by the way?"

"What was I supposed to say?"

"Well, you sat there agreeing with him."

"I did no such thing. How did I agree with him?"

"You kept saying things like, 'yeah' and 'sure," and 'I hear you,' when he was talking about the *dirty Japs*."

"It wasn't very pleasant for me either, Noriko. You heard him. He was three years out of combat. He fought at Okinawa, a regular bloodbath for the GI's. He is still pretty angry. Anything I said was not going to change his mind."

"I wasn't expecting you to change his mind," she said. "I was expecting you to ask him to stop talking like that or pull the cab over."

She sighed and returned her gaze to the window and said the first truly hurtful words in the 10 months we had been together. "I need a man with backbone, gaijin."

Ah, but backbone wasn't the issue, although mine was surely lacking.

It was another clue that Noriko, while comfortable being called an eccentric, would never abide being treated as an inferior or a commoner. Privilege had been her companion since birth; her family name granted her permission to be an oddity without societal condemnation, a rare set of circumstances in Japan where the opinion of society means everything.

She saw in America, even in the most inclusive of cities, that she would be a commoner or worse.

The relationship continued after returning to Japan but things weren't the same. Noriko's affections became erratic: passionate one day and distant the next. I began experiencing free-floating anxiety and, for the first time in my life, insomnia. I tried to get her to talk about why she wouldn't marry. She was evasive but finally, when pressed, used the classic Japanese expression: she was tangled up in *giri*, or the obligation to her family. And for some reason, I thought this explanation slippery, overly general, and without real substance. To my regret, I did not take it seriously.

XII
Into the archive

At the last minute, Noriko cancelled on a date to see a movie – *Treasure of the Sierra Madre* – saying the demands of work kept her.

I had worked furiously through the day to make time for this outing. By this time, I sensed our relationship was heading for a crash landing. I was desperate to salvage it any way I could. In disappointment, I skulked to Mrs. Ogawa's for the solace of sake. Except for a pair of businessmen getting quietly smashed at the small table, the place was empty.

Mrs. Ogawa read my mood. She brought a hot towel, heated up some good sake and fixed my two favorite snacks, *eihire* (fried sting ray fin) and *kimchee natto* (fermented soybeans and cabbage). She parked herself on her stool where she could keep an eye on her two other customers yet close enough to me so that we could speak quietly.

"Where's Noriko, Teddy?"

"We were supposed to go to a movie tonight."

"Is that so? And what happened?"

"She said she had too much work at NHK."

"Oh, that's pity. Well, she's a modern woman, so I suppose we can expect that sort of behavior."

I couldn't tell if Mrs. Ogawa was blaming me for unrealistic expectations or chastising Noriko for behaving rudely. By now I was so accustomed to Japanese ambiguity that I let the comment pass, telling myself I'd figure it out later.

"Her brother was in here the other day."

"Taki? Really? What was he doing here?"

"Business, I suppose. He was having sake with a very important person from government planning."

"I would have thought he had enough money to not worry about business."

"*Shihonkazei hōritsu* was very bad for Shibusawa family." she said, using the Japanese term for the Capital Levy Law, a one-time tax rammed through the Diet at SCAP's insistence meant to drain the coffers of the wealthy.

"Plus, you know us Japanese. Taki is obligated to do something to restore the family firm's reputation."

"What about their reputation needs restoring?" I asked, immediately regretting my straightforwardness.

Mrs. Ogawa looked over my shoulder at the two other patrons. "Excuse me," she said, as she moved off her perch. "I have obligations."

Well, that was that. I'd blown another chance to find out more about the Shibusawa family. I sighed and tucked into the kimchee, marveling at the sparkle of the pickled napa cabbage.

Yet Mrs. Ogawa returned to her stool. She refilled my cup. "You know this word, *gunbi*?" She asked it so softly I had to lean forward to hear.

"It means weapons of war. Armaments."

Mrs. Ogawa merely nodded at my translation. Then the connection came clear. "So," I asked, "the Shibusawa family made weapons for the imperial Army?"

Mrs. Ogawa bobbed her head again in affirmation, telling but not telling. She looked at the two men then back at me. "Special kind of weapon. Chemicals."

"What kind of chemicals?"

Mrs. Ogawa looked at the door as if she was ready to greet new customers. But no one was coming down the stairs. Still, without turning her head, she spoke as if addressing a ghost.

"The current occupiers of Japan are not so happy with the Shibusawa family. They have stripped many of the assets from the firm. Taki was in here talking to government official trying to reestablish a more," she paused, "acceptable path to being included in the rebuilding of Japan."

Then someone did come down the stairs, brushing past the valence curtain; Mrs. Ogawa came out from the behind the bar to bow and meet them.

###

The next morning, I pulled myself out of bed half an hour early, skipped my run, bath, and shave, threw on my uniform without checking in the mirror, and hustled to Dai-Ichi. I knew exactly who I was going to see.

Patterson L. Biggs was a button-down civilian lawyer from Charlottesville, Virginia. While he worked exclusively on anti-trust issues for the legal section, dismantling the *zaibutsu*, the Japanese conglomerates that fueled Japan's war machine, Biggs was the best-connected civvy in Dai-Ichi, his index file an object of envy. When he wasn't chained to his chair, he attended parties and functions, gathering gossip and scuttlebutt. I'd worked with him before and done him favors, doing last-minute translations late into the night. I enjoyed his company, envying his ambition, wit, and sharp mind, but learned that he did not tolerate fools.

Pursuing information about Noriko's family gave me the excuse to dig into something else that had gotten under my skin and wouldn't leave: Peter's death. The Legal section still wouldn't acknowledge they were investigating the fate of that B-29 crew, but body language and evasive replies told me they were stalling. If anyone would know what was up, it would be Biggs.

First, however, I had to get past Yamazaki-san, Biggs' bi-lingual secretary. She guarded her boss's access with more ferocity than any *komainu* or lion dog guarded a Shinto shrine. I knew she did not arrive before 7:30 while Biggs, a man who did not sleep more than a handful of hours, was often as his desk by 5:30. I knew I'd find him bent down over his desk, suit coat off, sleeves rolled up, Chesterfield butts already piled up in his ashtray.

To my satisfaction, the main door to his office swung open when I turned the knob. More pleasing was that Yamazaki-san's desk remained in shadow, chair neatly pulled up to the edge of the desk, and that the door to Bigg's office rested ajar, smoke-fused light shining through the open slit.

I knocked and simultaneously pushed opened the door. Biggs glanced up from his writing, cigarette between the fingers of one hand, foundation pen in the other, irritated at the interruption. But when he saw it was I, he set down his pen, grinned, stood and stuck out his hand.

"Well, my goodness," he said in his drawl. "If it isn't my favorite translator and doyen of all things Japanese. Have you come to offer your services? If so, I could most surely use them."

I shook his hand and my head simultaneously. "Sorry Biggs. As you southern boys would say, I'm otherwise indisposed. I just had a quick question about a certain company."

Biggs sat down and stubbed out his cigarette. "Right, then, Captain. Fire away."

The secret to dealing with Biggs was to treat him like an important asset who enjoyed giving out privileged information but also appreciate that his time was valuable. This man had important things to do. Get right to the point. I remained standing, as if to give the impression my query would only take a minute to answer.

"You know anything about a company called Shibusawa Trading?"

"Never heard of them," he said, his eyes flitting to a document on his desk.

"Really?"

Biggs pushed back in his chair, thinking. I couldn't tell if really considering the subject or making a show of studiousness. Then he shook his head.

"No, sir. I have no recollection of that company. What did they do?"

I tried again. "How about Takakichi Shibusawa?"

Patterson shook his head impatiently. I was wasting his time. He turned in his swivel chair to get something out of his in-box but stopped abruptly. He squinted his eyes, scrutinizing me, giving me a second look.

"Oh," he said, his voice descending. "*Mr*. Shibusawa. Taki. Oh, yes. Indeed."

I nodded my head. "And?"

"Interesting. Who wants to know?" he asked.

Not known for lightning-quick repartee, I fibbed. "I'm doing some translation and interpreting for the economic section. They have questions."

"Interesting," he said again. "Why don't you close that door and have a seat?"

I did so. "Well," he said then, as if to give himself time to parse his words, extracted a fresh pack of Chesterfields from his desk drawer, opened it – his Hampden-Sydney ring flashing in the light – shook one out, lit it, then set it in an ashtray.

"If someone hasn't told you this already, this subject is touchy. Very touchy. The legal and prosecution sections have their shorts in a serious wad over the matter. They're exceedingly tight lipped. Believe me, I've tried to gather more info but they keep us *zaibutsu* boys pretty much in the dark. But I have determined this much: the Shibusawa family owns a company once called Matataka Biological Products. Given your clearance, you probably know that the Japanese engaged in some pretty horrific experiments on prisoners, especially in Manchuria. Some of them involved subjecting prisoners to deadly bacterial and biological agents. Cholera. Typhus. That sort of delightful thing. Matataka manufactured at least some of those agents. Talk about aiding and abetting."

So, my interrogator's instinct had been right about Noriko fudging what her knowledge of the family business. I couldn't blame her, really.

"Are they going to be tried for war crimes?"

"Who? Matataka? Probably not. Actually, definitely not. Their name came up at the tribunal held at the JWM," he said, referring to the war trials held at the Japanese War Ministry auditorium, "but according to those in the know, the prosecution offered insufficient evidence. Matataka had seen the writing on the wall before the war ended and changed its name to Matataka Chemical, Ltd. They've done their best to cover their tracks. But they couldn't erase everything. There are plenty of people upstairs," he said, pointing towards the ceiling, "who want to see somebody from Matataka swing or at least pay dearly."

"And Taki?"

"Met him once. Have you?"

I said nothing.

"I have," said Biggs, "and I'm here to testify that he is one smooth and sophisticated operator. The word is he's using his charms and influence to pressure on various ministries to convince SCAP to back off Matataka's role. They've cleaned up. In fact, I heard the other day that Matataka wants a contract to supply cleaning solvents to bases down in Okinawa."

I wondered how much Noriko knew about this. It was hard to imagine she was completely unaware. But this development made me understand why she didn't want to discuss family matters.

I thanked him. "Now Biggs. I know you're busy but do you have just an extra minute?"

"For you, Captain, I do."

"I'm curious about something else also buried deep in Legal. What do you know about investigations into that B-29 that went down in Kyushu the day before the war ended?"

The question had an electrifying effect. Biggs sat bolt upright in his chair, spilling ash on his shirtsleeve. "Dear God, captain. That's what Legal calls case 330. How the hell did you even know they were looking into that matter? It's classified top secret."

"Well, I have my ways. But I'm not getting very far. What's the reason for this classification?

Biggs sat back in his chair, regained his composure, wiping the ash off his shirt. He took a deep draw of his cigarette and picked something off his lip that wasn't there. He exhaled, but kept the cigarette in his twitching fingers, waiting. Biggs wanted a quid pro quo. "Well, captain. You're two for two this morning, as far as looking into sensitive matters. But now I'm curious. What's up with your interest that fate of that B-29?"

"It's personal."

"How personal?"

"My brother, Sargent Peter Lundquist, was part of that crew and died at the hands of the Kempei Tai, or that's what the official report said. But the exact details remain confidential. I'd like to know more."

Biggs was not expecting this. He shook his head in empathy. "Good Lord, I had no idea," he said. Then he repeated himself: "Good Lord. My condolences, sir. Well, Captain, if your brother died in that incident, Legal needs to see you. I'm surprised they haven't put two and two together. I've heard they're trying to get the physical description of every man on the crew. What's your security clearance level?

"I've never been denied requests, except for this case 330, as you call it. I see all sorts of reports, as you might imagine."

"Indeed. Well, then, go straight to the top. "How do you get along with Carpenter?"

Biggs was referring to Colonel Alva C. Carpenter, head of SCAP's legal division.

"I've only had superficial interactions with him. I know his deputy pretty well, however."

"Richardson?"

"Yes."

"Have you tried him?"

"Yes. Not helpful."

"Well, sir. I'd try again. I'd tell him your brother was among the casualties."

The brown envelope arrived at my desk late in the afternoon. The courier was unusual in that it was MacArthur's right-hand man, General Bonner F. Fellers, a man who had never taken the time to personally darken the door of any aid-de-camp. If Fellers wanted to see you, you got a summons. But Fellers was on his way out. Retirement. Maybe he felt comfortable breaking protocol. Or maybe he went out of his way because he admired my ability to understand Japanese.

I rocketed out of my seat and saluted. Fellers closed the door and tugged on the knob to see if it was secured properly. The way he walked revealed his agitation. He stood in front of my desk. I offered him a chair but he declined. He held the envelope with both hands. I remained standing.

"As you were."

I sat.

"Next time you make a request from legal, captain, you go through official channels, meaning it begins at our office."

"Sir, I thought going through legal was the proper chain of command."

"Ordinarily, yes. But this situation is basically overseen by those above Colonel Carpenter's staff."

That meant MacArthur.

"Yessir."

He sighed. "Lundquist, you know damned well Mac's quandary over prosecutions. If he's overzealous, he'll be a vindictive despot. Yet too many war criminals get let off the hook and he'll get crucified in the press. And you know how sensitive he is about that. Your request for information about your brother's death created quite a stir. This is highly restricted. I myself had to approve the release. If you weren't direct kin, you'd never get to see this, no matter your security clearance level."

He plopped the envelope down on my desk. "This is the summary of what we know so far. The actual file is hundreds of pages and growing. "This," Fellers said, putting his index finger on the envelope, "doesn't leave your office. Gets locked up when you leave and needs to be back in my office at 0800 hours tomorrow."

"Yessir. I appreciate you going to bat for me. Sir, if it's possible, can you tell me why this document has such a high clearance level?"

Fellers hesitated. "There are two reasons, captain. The Russians are looking into atrocities committed by the Japanese in Manchuria related to biological warfare."

"As in the Pingfan Laboratory, sir?"

"That's correct, captain. Moscow's clamoring for every piece of evidence we have concerning Pingfan. In case you haven't heard, we don't like the Russians or their agenda. We think they're scheming to use what happened at Pingfan as an excuse to wring more concessions from the Japanese. They're probably going to get Sakhalin and the Kurils but intelligence tells us they're shooting for Hokkaido. We absolutely want Hokkaido to stay part of Japan. Secondly, Kyushu Imperial University has direct ties to the Imperial Palace and the Emperor. If there is any evidence that the Imperial Palace was aware of what went on at the medical school in Kyushu – which is where your brother ended up – it opens up the avenue for the Emperor to be declared a war criminal. Australia has already done that. As you know, Mac thinks that's a very, very bad objective. Lastly, everything that was done to your brother happened after the war officially ended. That creates complications. Any more questions, captain?"

"No, sir. Thank you."

His shoulders relaxed just a bit and he glanced out the window behind me. "I don't blame you for wanting more details. I'd do the same if I were in your shoes. But I've got to warn you, Lundquist. This summary doesn't spare the macabre particulars. These guys were worse than Mengele."

I stood and again saluted. Fellers left, leaving the door open.

I sat down. For a long time, I just stared at the envelope, asking myself if I really wanted to see what was inside. Finally, I turned on my desk light and opened the flap of the envelope. I withdrew a folder marked *Case 330. Summary as of March 3rd, 1946. Top Secret*.

Peter's B-29 was shot down over Miyazaki prefecture, located in the southern half of Kyushu. Laced with gorges, it's rugged and mountainous. Only by a miracle did anyone survive. Five crew members, including the captain, didn't. Those who managed to crawl out of the wreckage found themselves surrounded by farmers with scythes and shotguns. They shot and killed one of the crewmen. The remainder were bound and brought to the local office of the Kempei Tai, the equivalent of the Japanese Gestapo.

Another crew member, badly injured by the crash, died at the lands of the Kempei Tai. A First Lieutenant named Toji Kentaro had lost his mother in a raid on Fukuoka the previous week and sought revenge. His superiors granted him his wish. Toji cut off the airman's head.

On the third day of their captivity, the surviving men were driven 160 miles from Miyazaki to Karume, headquarters of the Kyushu Kempei Tai.

The following day they were transported to Fukuoka, home of Kyushu Imperial University. The date – August 14, 1945 – is significant. Japan officially surrendered that day. The four men should have been released.

Instead, they were used as medical guinea pigs. The doctors injected the quartet with seawater, which they hypothesized could be used as temporary blood substitute. All four lived through the experiment, despite a near lethal drop in blood pressure. Then the vivisection became aggressive. One of the attending physicians, Hirao Kenichi, testified to two brain operations, a stomach removal, a liver operation, and one lung experiment.

In his written confession, Hirao said the surgeons had noted Peter's athletic build and singled him out for the lung experiment. They sedated him, removed a lung, then sewn him back up. They marveled at how his oxygen levels remained relatively constant.

Then it dawned on the staff of Kyushu Imperial University that the Marines now stationed at Itazuke Airbase outside of Fukuoka were just the start of a rapidly mobilizing occupation.

I held my breath as I read the next paragraph. Peter was again sedated and his chest opened up. An assistant surgeon, unidentified, reached in and manually stopped that massive heart.

I shut the folder, numb, unable to read any further. But then curiosity about what happened to the body made me take a second look. The staff of the medical school cremated the bodies of all four airman; the ashes were thrown in a heap in back of the crematorium.

I never told my parents about what really happened. Nor did we have a discussion when in 1949 the news came out with some of the details about Kyushu. Even that account was censored heavily. The trial made clear the names of the Japanese involved. However, of the eleven men who went down with Peter's B-29, it was never revealed until 40 years later who died upon impact of the crash, who was shot by local farmers, what man died at the hands of the Kempei Tai, and who perished on the operating table during vivisection. The military kept that all under wraps.

My parents asked no questions. My stepmother started going to mass every day. My father nightly retreated to his study, spending evenings under the anesthesia of brandy. During the weekend he puttered about the greenhouse. The American Legion tried to get him to join. "Not at gunpoint," he said, apparently without irony.

Noriko vanished. Wouldn't pick up her phone at work or her apartment. Nobody answered when I knocked on her door. Noriko's boss at NHK told me she had taken an official leave of absence due to illness. He didn't know when she would return. Desperation set in. I found the number to Shibusawa Trading and repeatedly tried to reach Taki. He was never there and refused to return my calls. Didn't dare contact her parents.

I kept telling myself she would resurface any day but my gut told me otherwise. I got it in my head that Noriko was sneaking back to her apartment at night, the logic of hopelessness. One evening I went to Mrs. Ogawa's and got so drunk she refused to pour me one more cup, a first. Then I went to Noriko's apartment and broke down the door.

Three months later, my commission expired and I returned to stateside, temporarily to Idaho, with the sword amongst my possessions.

XIII
Rising Sun

We reached a compromise. Sylvia would fly with me as far as Hawaii then I would go on to Japan alone. But she wasn't the kind of gal who would sit alone by the pool, sipping umbrella drinks while her husband went afield to settle old romantic accounts. No, sir. She had an acquaintance from the legal realm (she has these friends all over the globe) who invited her to go for a three-day sail from Maui to Oahu. Sylvia was so excited by the thought of sailing again I thought she completely forgot about my mission. But in the bed we shared before she climbed aboard her friend's 48-footer and I ducked into another plane for a long flight to Osaka, Sylvia spooned me and, whispering in my ear, quoting the Sonnet of Fidelity from the Brazilian poet, Vinicius de Moraes:

Above all, to my love I'll be attentive
First and always, with care and so much
That even when facing the greatest enchantment
By love be more enchanted my thoughts.

###

I, who know nothing about swordcraft, long thought the sword radiated an ancient temper that even the most talented modern forger would struggle to emulate. The two customs agents at Osaka International apparently agreed. The mottled tempering marks on the blade convinced them of its age.

"Hijo ni furuidesu" or very old, said the senior of the two inspectors. To my surprise, they didn't even dissemble the handle to look at the signature of the maker. Their concern centered on the approximate – the operative term – age of the sword and that it had not been forged in Korea or Spain. A post-WWII foreign-made knock-off would have disqualified the sword from receiving a temporary import permit.

For once I was grateful for Nick's compulsive thoroughness. Upon learning that I had made the decision to personally take the sword back, Nick got someone at the US embassy staff in Tokyo to contact the port police at Osaka International. They had been apprised of my mission and the date of my arrival. No downside to that over functioning. Connections matter in Japan, particularly on culturally sensitive issues like this one.

However, more importantly, and on a practical basis, Nick had found the address of the Kyoto *Shinsa* and the time and date they meet. Since they only gathered on the second Tuesday of every month, this was a key piece of information. Thankfully Nick pointed this out before I booked tickets. Moreover, in order to be issued a temporary import permit, I had to know this information, telling the port police exactly what day I would appear before the Shinsa.

Taking no chances that I would go gallivanting around the land of the rising sun with the sword, the port police gave me an import permit that expired in one week. Connections or no, when it came to matters concerning ancient samurai swords, it was all business in Japan.

A wave of exhaustion washed over me as I re-wrapped the sword and the younger of the port policeman wrote out the import permit. Being burdened with the inability to sleep on airplanes, I had not closed my eyes in 20 hours. I could not wait to get to my hotel room, sink into a tub of piping hot water to sooth my contracting back, indulge in a well-deserved tumbler of scotch, then crawl into bed. I did exactly that after I telephoned Sylvia, using the SAT phone number she gave me, in Hawaii and telling her I had safely arrived.

It's odd what you worry about when you're old, like the firmness of a hotel mattress. Yet the Sheraton Miyako provided the ideal bed, albeit too short: a delicious blend of firm but cushy on the top. I was happy and relieved that I had acquired my temporary transport permit. In my checklist mind, I had just ticked-off an important task.

I fell into a dreamless state then awoke when it was still dark, having no idea of the time, drowsy from the allergy meds (help me stay asleep) and the muscle relaxants. I felt a surge of energy and arose and wrapped myself in the complimentary high-tread count cotton yukata which, of course, was far too short, the hem rakishly above the knee.

I felt the first real hunger, verging on ravenous. Even though the clock revealed it was 4:07, I put my hearing aids in and telephoned room service for breakfast. With typical Japanese alacrity, it arrived promptly, delivered by a shadow of a girl not a day over 20 who professed polite astonishment that some old round-eye could prattle on with her in Japanese. She could not suppress a giggle, hand clamped over her mouth, at the misfit of my yukata but, what the hell, we laughed together. I had to take a minute to appreciate the artfully arranged meal set on a vermillion lacquered tray: raw egg over hot rice, a fantastic red miso soup, grilled salmon, nori, pickles, and green tea. I wished Diego was there so I could have given him the skin from my salmon.

I ran a bath for my morning soak. My bathtub played *ava maria* to inform me that the water had finished filling and was waiting for me. Had a second cup of tea, then watched the sun come up over the sprawl of Osaka.

I thought about calling Alice then reconsidered. As she told me one time, "when you go down to the river, watching it flow and ask yourself the really important questions in life, you have to go down there alone."

There was one call I could not put off: Noriko. Still apprehensive and nervous, I decided to follow my daily routine and take a walk. It was a clear fall day, crisp with no rain in the immediate forecast, the time between autumn and snow, as Noriko had said so many years ago.

Thoreau said that dawn brings back the heroic age; I especially appreciate early morning as a big city awakens. I take pleasure in watching deliveries and shopkeepers opening up their stores, sweeping the walks in front of their homes, seeing the breakfast street vendors set up as the sunlight glints off telephone lines, all without the constant shoulder to shoulder crowds one finds in most Asian cities. Moreover, I could feel my brain engage and congratulated myself that I could still read all of the street signs and understood most of the passing conversation. I didn't feel quite so damned antediluvian.

As I walked, I marveled, as I invariably do each time I return to Japan, how a country can rise from the ashes of war to create such vitality.

I returned to the hotel, collected myself, took a few deep breaths, and dialed her number.

Noppo? she asked after she picked up and I told her who it was. Her voice still had growling squeak. "I cannot believe I'm hearing your voice. Are you in Japan?"

"Osaka. I arrived last night."

"*Sou desuka*," she said,

"Did you make the journey alone?" which was Japanese way of asking if I was married and if I was, did I bring my wife along?

"It was a solo trip, Noriko."

"Well," she said as if expecting this answer. "It's a constant solo life for me, Noppo, as a widow."

I felt a little lightheaded. How the hell did this happen? In less than 20 seconds, we had established that I was in Japan alone and Noriko was a widow. The bonfire had been properly prepped and arranged. All it would take was a match to ignite a blaze. A part of me could barely be restrained from telling her that I had booked a room at an exquisite ryokan in Kyoto that night – one with an ancient and exquisite plum tree in the courtyard. Could she come join me for dinner?

Reality gave me the boot. The last time Sylvia and I had something resembling sex was three years ago and it took a double dose of Viagra and a damned lot of coaxing and patience on her behalf.

Noriko must have taken my silence as a cue to switch subjects. "Give me your hotel fax number, Noppo. I want to send you a map."

One or one hundred riders, the interior of Japan trains are as quiet as the waiting room of a morgue. No boomboxes or hawkers. People talking quietly or reading, particularly manga comics. It's almost like flying except the seats are damn sight more comfortable.

Although Kyoto was only an hour's train ride from Osaka, I gave myself a full day to make the journey. I wanted to relish each step. The ryokan I had reserved in Kyoto was ungodly expensive. I had stayed there once years ago on a business trip but this time no expense account was going to cover my costs. I rationalized this was going to be my last visit to Japan, not an occasion to be a budget traveller. I slept poorly. The futon wasn't all that comfortable, plus I was nervous about appearing before the Shinsa the next day. I worked on my speech.

I'd had already gone over it a dozen times but still felt anxious.

I had a bit of a fright the next morning when I arrived at the building that housed the Shinsa. The taxi pulled up in front of an off-yellow imposing brick structure that looked like it was designed on Versailles. This couldn't be the Kyoto Prefectural Office. I'd looked at the address I'd written down, wondering if my aging brain had played tricks on me.

"What is this place? I asked aloud, almost to myself.

I saw the driver looking at me in the rearview mirror. I don't imagine he understood the question, but grasped something might be amiss.

I asked him if this was indeed the correct address, making sure to let him know that perhaps I, not he, had made a mistake. He was trim and tanned, probably from getting bargain tee time rates in late fall. He turned to look at me in his immaculately pressed white shirt, dark blue textured tie, and obligatory cap. "So sorry to ask but are you here for matters concerning the registration of katana?"

When the driver picked me up at the ryokan, I noticed him looking at what I was carrying. Hard to imagine it being anything but a sword.

"I am."

He smiled broadly, happy to be the bearer of good news, and announced that this was indeed where the Shinsa met. This is the old Kyoto prefectural office, he explained, pointing out the window, but now it's a museum. "It's still used for meetings," he said and added for emphasis, "official meetings."

Over the years, he said, he had brought many sword-bearing passengers to this destination. "Just go through the doors to the central office. They will escort you to the designated room."

Indeed, a pimply young man with horn-rim glasses at the main desk led me up a set of stairs to a beautifully spacious room, amply lit by a bank of east-facing small pane windows. I was expecting a stuffy, windowless room of a municipal bureaucracy complete with fluorescent lights. Instead, the warmth of the room bolstered my confidence. Two tables, one larger than the other, sat in front of about 20 folding chairs, about half of them occupied by people with swords. I was the only non-Japanese petitioner. Five men, none younger than 70, sat at the larger table, tea cups at the ready. At the smaller table sat a younger man, a secretary or assistant, I supposed. In front of him lay several stacks of paper and a *mekuginuki,* a small brass hammer used to dissemble sword handles.

I went to the central table, bowed, said my name, and asked for a registration form. The men simultaneously bobbed their heads. The man sitting in the center chair, obviously the major domo, motioned for me to get the necessary paperwork from the assistant. I did so.

The assistant examined my passport, import permit, then asked me to fill out the registration form. Because my skill in writing had waned, I filled out my name in Japanese then asked him if he would fill out the form as I dictated the information to him. He studied me just long enough to be at the edge of violating a Japanese etiquette against staring, then said of course.

Two sections of the application caused him pause. One was on the maker and age of the sword. I told him I didn't know but I had reason to believe it was made in the Muromachi period and that it probably came from the forge of Muramasa Sengo, "but probably not Muramasa himself," I added cautiously.

"Really?" he said, trying to be polite and cover up his opinion that this was gaijin fantasy. "How interesting. Well, we'll see when it comes time for sword inspection."

Secondly, he asked me how I had acquired the sword. Here, I gambled on outright honesty. "I regret to say, I stole this sword from a household during occupied Japan."

At first he didn't believe me. "It was not a gift or a war souvenir?"

"No, it was neither. It was stolen. I will be more than willing to tell the whole story before the Shinsa."

"Yes. That would probably be best if you did that," he said. "And what was the name of the person from whom you stole the sword."

"It was a member of the Shibusawa family."

The secretary gave an undisguised guttural utterance of astonishment and, for the first time, I think he believed me.

"Is that so? And are you here to return the sword to a member of that family?"

"I am."

"And what is his name, please?"

"It's her and her name. Her maiden name was Noriko Shibusawa. She is the daughter of Takeshe Shibusawa. Her married name is Noriko Tomonosuke."

"I see. And is Mrs. Tomonosuke aware that you are returning the sword? Have you been in correspondence?"

"Yes."

"When do you plan to return this sword?"

I almost said, "tomorrow," but modified my answer to: "if my application for registering this sword is granted, then I will return it tomorrow."

"Will Mrs. Tomonsuke be there in person to receive the sword?"

"Yes."

"And, please, what is her address?"

All this back and forth between a gaijin and the assistant attracted attention from shinza board. They were listening while not pretending they were listening.

Finally, the secretary gave me a number and said to appear before the board when it was called. Bring the sword directly to him, he said. It needed to be unwrapped and ready to be dissembled.

I waited as others with swords went before the board. Some only took five minutes, other as much as 20. The committee took a break.

Finally, they called my number. I adjusted my tie and stood, feeling wretchedly nervous.

As instructed, I brought the sword unwrapped to the assistant, set it on his desk and bowed. The assistant placed the sword directly in front of him and waited. Then I stepped in front of the Shinsa and bowed very deeply, unmistakably an act of contrition, hoping the action would set the tone of my registration process.

Five heads nodded back.

They asked to see my temporary import permit then the application for registration.

"Now," said the chairman, after the papers had passed back and forth, "please tell us how you came to be in possession of this sword?"

I pursed my parched lips and I chose words that, in a language laced with ambiguity and double entendre, carried clear and explicit meaning: contrition, clearing the honor of a family name, and acceptance of responsibility. I began slowly, strangely confident of my Japanese.

"Thank you for the opportunity to appear before this board. My name is Theodore Lundquist. I am 80 years old. I am an American and was stationed as an Army officer to Tokyo from 1946 to 1948. Through an unfortunate incident, I stole a sword from the apartment of a member of the Shibusawa family. It was a dishonorable act I have regretted all my life. Now, I have come back to Japan to return the sword to its rightful owners, give my apologies and hopefully restore some honor back to the family. I ask your indulgence in registering this katana so I may fulfill my obligations."

The men stared back at me. I thought my plan had gone awry. Then the chairman said, in a chipper fashion: "Your Japanese is very commendable. We will certainly look into this situation. Let us inspect the sword first."

It might have been my imagination, but my speech seemed to infuse the room with an air of excitement.

First the men looked at the sword unsheathed, passing it back and forth. Then they took the sword out of the scabbard and examined the scabbard and the sword separately. Then they handed the sword back to the assistant.

"Will you please disassemble the sword so we might examine the tang?"

The assistant, *mekuginuki* at ready, immediately took up the task. With speed and precision, he removed the handle, then the *tsuba*, or guard, then the *seppa* and the *habaki*. Four of the five board members watched him in action. The fifth, however, kept glancing back at me. I began to worry that my presentation had been too frank and possibly offensive. I had noticed this gentleman right away. He was short, even by Japanese standards, and pear-shaped, and wore a loud double-breasted suit more fitting for a Ginza stroll in Tokyo than sword-inspecting body in old Kyoto. His hair was immaculate, not a gray hair out of place. Designer glasses rest snuggly against the bridge of his nose.

As the sword went back and forth among the board, as did the *tsuba, seppa,* and *habaki*, they obviously gave their pudgy cohort deference. His opinion commanded authority and much to my relief, after about 20 minutes of discussion, he announced that sword was not made by Muramasa Sengo, but mostly likely by one of his students. If they had reached the conclusion that Sengo himself had forged the blade, it would have been requisitioned as a National Treasure.

Still, the chairman said, "this is the oldest blade we've seen in recent memory. No major *kizu* (flaws), either. We grant registration of this sword and greatly appreciate its return to Japan," he said. They handed the blade back to the assistant for reassembly.

###

I walked back to my chair in a daze, wrung out and relieved. I had to wait until the end of the session to receive the registration document plus I was obliged to pay the registration fee, about $2,000. If the sword had been rejected, I would be required to pay only half that price. When the last petitioner sat down in his chair, the session was over. I paid my fee from a wad of ¥10,000 notes and picked up my precious registration form. Various applicants approached me and shook my hand, offering congratulations. I was making for the door when the pear-shaped gentlemen from the Shinsa panel appeared at my side. In formal and polite Japanese, he bowed and proffered a business card with both hands, which read, *Kazuma Sugimoto, collector*.

Collect what? I wondered, but that was for me to figure out by virtue of nuanced conversation, something I was in no mood to do. My gut told me this guy wanted something. What did I care? I was trying to be polite but was exhausted and wanted to get back to the ryokan so I could take a nap. My back was starting to throb.

Sugimoto sensed this lack of interest. Yet protocol dictated he couldn't rush things. Only when it might look like the conversation would end did he make his purpose known.

"Pardon me for being so forward, but could you take the trouble to have lunch with me?"

"Today?" I asked, trying to sound polite but uninterested at the same time.

"Yes, please, that is what I had in mind, if it's not too much of an inconvenience. I shall not keep you long."

I desperately wanted to decline but something about this man's request and a latent sense of perseverance made me accept.

"I am grateful," he said, "please excuse me while I call my driver."

He extracted a cellular telephone, something nobody in our age bracket in Flagstaff ever touched, from his inner coat pocket, uttered a few words, then closed the phone. "Please," he said, gesturing for me walk with him.

We had waited no more than 30 seconds at the curb of this mini-Versailles when a recent-model dark green Bentley turbo with a uniformed driver stopped in front of us. I reassessed my situation. Who the hell *was* this guy? This could turn out to be complicated. We were whisked away, the beamy Bentley navigating the narrow ancient streets with remarkable agility. Sugimoto again apologized and took out his cell phone. When the party answered, he simply said, "Sugimoto, number eight," then closed the phone.

He turned to me. "Again, thank you for allowing me to meet with you on such short notice. My club is just five minutes away. You were very brave, very honorable today, Mr. Lundquist."

"You are too polite. Not really."

"No. No. I know something about the katana business and you absolutely did the right thing. The committee was very impressed with your presentation. You could have mailed that sword and be done with it. Instead, you appeared in person. You understand the Japanese, Mr. Lundquist. You are fortunate the press did not hear of this story. They would have swarmed all over you."

I hadn't thought of that. "Yes, I'm grateful I didn't have to deal with that. So, you collect swords?"

He smiled, a curve in a marshmallow face. "Oh, I collect many things, Mr. Lundquist, many things. Swords are just one of them. But, I did not ask you for lunch to discuss the sword."

Totally flummoxed, I bobbed my head in acknowledgment of his statement, regretting I had accepted his invitation, and tried to figure out the most polite way to ask what he wanted. The hum of Bentley's tires, alternated between a quiet purr when going over old paving stones and a barely audible hiss when the rubber hit pavement.

The Bentley slowed and abruptly turned into an alley and stopped in front of a modest single-story dark gray stucco building. The driver hopped out and opened my door and stood at attention. I exited, carrying the sword, and the driver shut the door then ran around the car to see to Sugimoto's door. The Bentley drove away. We found ourselves standing in front of an aged polished teak door surrounded by a black frame. Sugimoto attended to the keypad on the righthand side of the door. There was a faint buzzing sound and Sugimoto opened the door and gestured for me enter.

We were expected. A bespectacled wiry middle-aged man in a starched butler's uniform, who had a startlingly similar resemblance to the deceased Emperor Hirohito, met us in an anti-room, bowed and took our coats, mine first. When he saw the wrapped sword, his eyes momentarily met with Sugimoto's, who made a faint grunt, a sign that the sword was to stay in my hands. A waiter, dressed in black pants and white shirt and black bow tie, suddenly appeared. Sugimoto pulled the waiter aside for a brief consult then made a motion for me to follow the employee. Sugimoto tread close behind.

I was in new territory. Throughout the years of doing business in Japan, I'd been in private clubs, mostly owned by corporations, but I'd only read about places like this: a refuge for ultra-wealthy men. We passed a bar, which looked half-full, and through the side of a dining room, of which there were only a few patrons. No one looked up or even glanced at us. That would have been indiscreet. No women. It was so dark I could barely see and was grateful for the waiter's white shirt.

The waiter led us through another door and into a passageway with doors on either side. He stopped at the open door with the symbol for the number, eight – *hachi* – painted in elegant calligraphy on the frame.

The waiter turned, bowed and waited for us to enter. A windowless room, surprisingly well lit, laid out in classic Japanese design of tatami mats, ancient prints of trees and birds, and calligraphic scrolls awaited us. We took off our shoes. My back spasmed as I bent over. Thank Christ the dark table, about two feet off the floor, had a space underneath it so diners could sit western-style, feet able to touch the floor, as opposed to obliging a kneeling or cross-legged sitting position. My old bones couldn't accommodate such positions for long. It would be enough of a challenge to get down on the mat.

"Please. Sit," said Sugimoto. I managed, gingerly, slowly, to oblige. Sugimoto did not put his legs under the table, but instead knelt on the tatami.

Thirty seconds later, the waiter returned and placed a bottle of Glen Grant Whisky on the table. A red banner across the label announced the whisky was casked in 1937, the year I graduated high school in Pocatello. The waiter added a pair of glasses to the table, then disappeared. I stared at the array in dismay. I'm not much of a day drinker. Besides, this was not a casual gesture. Something important was in the offing. For the life of me, I could not anticipate what was coming.

Sugimoto read my concern. "Please, do not worry. I only ask you to take a thimble of this."

Glittering beads of sweat appeared on Sugimoto's forehead, out of exertion maybe but I suspected anxiety. He produced an ironed off-white cotton handkerchief from inside his coat pocket and patted his brow. The waiter reappeared with tray of *otsumami*, the petite appetizers I'd relished at Mrs. Ogawas. But they were exquisitely arranged on gleaming porcelain of a quality I've never seen outside private homes. The waiter disappeared. The room went silent but for the hum of a far-off air conditioning unit and Sugimoto's labored breathing.

Sugimoto gently uncorked the bottle and poured a lovely golden barley-colored inch in my glass. His hands shook slightly. After he stopped I, without thinking, I took the bottle from him and poured him an equal portion in his glass.

Sugimoto's eyes went soft, appreciative of my following simple Japanese etiquette. I waited for him to lift his glass, but he did not. He let out a deep breath.

"Again, thank you for accepting my invitation. When I saw your name on the form to register the sword, I thought the gods were playing tricks on me. But when you told us the story of how you acquired the sword, I knew the fates meant business."

Sugimoto fingered the glass nervously, turning it slowly. "If I am not mistaken, Mr. Lundquist, you had a brother, a brother named Peter. Please. Am I correct?

I felt as if a sumo wrestler had landed on my chest. This was absolutely the last thing I was expecting.

I nodded my head. "Yes, I did."

"And he was killed in the war? Killed in Japan? Am I also correct?"

I wanted to say, 'in a manner of speaking,' but instead I just said yes.

Sugimoto looked at the table and gave a deep fatalistic sigh.

"*Sore wa sōdesu,*" he said. It is so.

He spoke a low voice, almost a whispered baritone. "When I was sitting at the Shinsa committee and realized who was before me, I could scarcely keep my mind on the business at hand. Katanas were suddenly nothing. Nothing! My brain was racing; I was mostly trying to decide if I had the courage to delve into this matter of your brother. I finally decided that I must seize this chance, for surely the gods will never give me another opportunity. Again, I thank you."

"And what do you know about my brother?" I ventured to ask.

He took a sip of his whisky, signaling that it was all right for me to do the same. I don't know if it was the drama of the moment but it tasted like kaopectate. Sugimoto shifted on his knees.

"You see, Mr. Lundquist, in the year 1945, I was a first-year medical student at Kyushu Imperial University."

I did in involuntary intake of breath and took another sip of whisky for something to do.

"And although I had nothing to do with the heinous fashion your brother, or any member of that B-29 crew died, everyone in the medical school knew what happened. The school tried to keep it a secret but that," he paused, "of course, was not possible. Besides, all the details came out in the Tokyo trial. For all the world to see. The shame of Japan. And it was made all the worse because eventually, every one of those involved in those crimes got their sentences commuted and were set free."

He slowly shook his head and gave a deep half-grunt, half-sigh, a sign of disapproval right out of a Kurosawa movie. "That incident made me ashamed to be in medicine. Of course, to please my parents, I completed medical school and become a physician. But when they died, I gave up my license to practice. Besides, I found real estate speculation much to my liking and much more profitable than medicine. Compared to your country, physicians in Japan are shockingly underpaid."

He frowned and waved his hand, like he was trying to bat away that last statement about money, as if it were too unseemly.

Sugimoto got to his feet, grunting with the effort. His pudgy frame wobbled a little and, for the briefest moment, he touched the table top for balance. Then he clasped his arms by his side. Then he bowed low, his upper frame almost parallel with the table top, remarkably low for such man burdened with a substantial gut. He easily bowed as low as I had before the Shinsa.

"On behalf of people of Japan, I wish to apologize for what happened to your brother. What we did was unconscionable. We have no excuse. It is my sincere hope that this inadequate gesture will somehow ease your family's pain."

Sugimoto used "*owabi*", the most formal term for issuing an apology. It's a serious word in Japan, one with no haziness. Moreover, in classic Japanese fashion, he personally burdened himself with the gruesome actions of a nation at war; the cause of Peter's death was not the work of one person and all Japanese were in some way responsible. He also affirmed that Peter's death did not just effect me.

He only stopped bowing when his designer glasses started to fall off.

I should have stood, but I was too overcome. I bowed sitting down. My head fell forward of its own accord. It stayed there, tears falling into the ancient whiskey and table. I should have said something like formal, such as, *shitsurei shimasu.*

But I all I could manage was, *ii n desu.* That's OK.

I remember very little about the taxi ride back to the ryokan. It was like waking up after surgery. I have vague memories of stopping to buy a bottle of expensive sake that came in an elegant wooden box. I recall standing in my spare understated quarters overlooking a rock garden, sword in hand. I wanted to talk to Sylvia or Alice or someone about what had just happened, but lacked the will to go through the front desk and organize an international call. Sylvia would be worried or worse, not having heard from me since the first night I landed. I was surprised she hadn't called me as she had my itinerary and number of the ryokan.

I recall clutching the outside of my suit jacket pocket for the sword registration, just checking to see if it was still there. I took off my coat and I kicked off my shoes without untying them then lay down in the fetal position on the firm bed.

I awoke with a start, sweating, and, as in the Sheraton two nights ago, had no idea of the time. Still dark, moonlight cascading through my window. Normally a restless sleeper having to adjust my position to ease various pains – my back freezes up about two hours in the same position – I had slept on my right side without moving an inch. I was very thirsty. No bedside clock. I got up. When I stood I was vaguely dizzy, feeling stiff and fuzzy. I found my glasses. I looked my watch: 3:50. I'd slept for over 15 hours. It was the first time I'd slept in my clothes since I stole the sword half a century ago. I still had my earing aides in. One of them had run out of juice. I had to pee badly but, as it does from time to time with old men, I couldn't. I had FloMax in my Dopp kit and washed down a tablet. I wish I had followed Silvia's advice and brought my emergency Foley catheter. Luckily, I remembered my urologist advice that soaking in a hot bath can relax the prostate, at least enough so it will stop blocking up the works.

I ran the hottest bath I could stand. It did the trick.

The last thing I'd put in my stomach was vintage scotch. I'd eaten practically nothing of Sugimoto's offerings. The ryokan mini bar thankful produced an ice-cold bottle of water, a bag of peanuts and a Japanese Kit-kat bar. I ate and took another bath and sat there thinking about Noriko then Peter then back to Noriko. As the water warmed my stiff joints and bones, I remembered Noriko's letter and how she said she was an early riser. I wasn't supposed to meet her until nine that morning. I wanted this ordeal to end. But why not call and see if she could meet me earlier?

Naked, I dialed her number. The phone rang five times and I was about to hang up when she answered.

"Noriko. It's Teddy," I said softly, not wanting to wake the other guests in the ryokan. "Good morning. I'm sorry to call you at this hour. I'm sure I got you out of bed."

She gave that squeaky laugh. "On the contrary, Noppo. I have been up for hours. I'm very excited to see you."

"Well, I was wondering if we needed to wait until nine o'clock?"

"I have no objection to an early gentleman caller," she said. "What time would you like to come?"

"How about in an hour or around six o'clock?"

"That suits me very well. Have you had breakfast?"

Before I could answer, she said. "Of course you haven't. Good. I'll prepare some. And good green tea. How does that sound?"

"That sounds very nice."

"Good, I'll see you shortly. And you have my address?"

"I do."

"And the map I faxed you?"

"Yes."

"Right-o," she rasped cheerfully and hung up. It was if half a century had never passed.

I went back to the minibar and fetched an ice coffee. I needed caffeine to help me figure out what time it was in Hawaii. Mid-morning the previous day, an ideal time to call.

Sylvia answered on the first ring.

"Teddy?" she asked, as if she had clairvoyant powers as to the identity of the caller. One word bespoke of relief and anger.

"Hi, Sylvia."

"Are you all right?" I could tell this was not going to be conversation guided by reason and calm.

"I'm fine, I think. It's been quite a day."

"What do you mean, you think? Are you OK or not? Is there some reason you haven't called me earlier?"

"Sylvia. I'm not sure I can explain just what happened to me."

"Oh," I heard her voice rise. "Do I want to hear the rest of his conversation? Do I need to book a flight back to Flagstaff flying solo?"

Then she uttered, "*o bastardo*," on the intake of a breath, faint but distinct.

I thought for sure I'd hear the receiver go dead.

"Sylvia. Please. I haven't even seen Noriko yet. You know my itinerary."

There was a pause but she didn't hang up.

"Then why haven't you called?"

Instead of employing a lame defensive tactic, like "it's only been a day, Sylvia," I reminded myself that this was a woman who was putting a good face and being brave and logical but could no longer deny the feeling of a looming threat. Sylvia had an excellent bullshit detector and I knew she would find assurance in clarity and honesty.

"Well, would you like to hear the full story?"

"Do you have time for that?" she asked sarcastically, still not convinced I hadn't seen Noriko on the sly.

"Yes, indeed I do." Noriko could wait.

###

She lived in Higashiyama, the oldest section of Kyoto, a warren of winding, narrow, stone-covered streets. Figuring out street addresses in Japan can stump the cleverest minds; Kyoto, which uses a grid-based system for address, was known for having the most byzantine system of all. Many streets don't even have names. The taxi driver dropped me off where the streets got even more constricted. By Noriko's map, I reckoned to be about three blocks from her home. I would have preferred to be driven to her door but the driver, apologizing, pointed to a sign prohibiting cars or trucks. Only delivery motorcycles were permitted.

She didn't say anything about that.

In Japan, the taxi drivers control the back doors. When my driver closed mine, the thump triggered the collapse of defenses I'd maintained ever since I ducked into the plane in Honolulu. My immunity was low. I was insufficiently recovered from my luncheon with Sugimoto and I felt off-kilter and vulnerable. The rain, more like a mist, and the distinctive sound of someone behind a wall walking in getas, wooden flip-flops – a rhythmic clap, clap, clap – pulled me into the vortex of old Japan. The brassy smell of rain on granite mixed with the scent of decaying leaves reminded me of the first night Noriko and I had spent together. There was a dank in the air that made me want to drink warm sake. Yes, I could hear modern sounds: jets and the hum of the city beyond these quiet streets but they didn't take away from my trance.

A bicycle bell – *bring, bring* – a timeless sound, as prevalent now as it was in 1948, came from a distant somewhere. The faint drizzle coated the stones and manhole covers, making them gleam as if polished. I wished I'd brought a walking stick. Fortunately, suspecting rain, I'd taken advantage of the ryokan's collection of loanable umbrellas. Still, for the sake of the sword, which had no waterproof covering, I hoped to find Noriko's house without delay.

 I pushed onward, more like a fast shuffle.

I past a bent old woman, ignoring the mist, sweeping the street in front of her house. Her mother's mother's mother swept the same volcanic dust on the same street using a similar broom. She looked up, nodded, and went about her business. The light, defuse with mist, had not come up above the buildings, when I found her home. It was as she described: the only house inset from the street. A set of wooden doors, which swung open from the center, were placed in the middle of ancient stucco wall. It gave the place a distinctly aristocratic touch. The doors were not locked Noriko had said. Just push through, walk through the front garden and knock at the main door.

I did so. Almost immediately, the door opened, just a crack, as if the occupant was waiting for me to push it open, then it widened almost all the way.

And there she was, smiling, looking up at me from a wheelchair. Her silver hair was pulled austerely back into a tight bun. Age had tucked her face a bit. She had put on lipstick and eye shadow. And although she wore a trace of face powder, it couldn't hide her freckles.

If she noticed the shock on my face at seeing her in a wheelchair, she pretended not to notice it.

"Oh, Noppo," Noriko gushed and clasped her hands together. "You came! I was afraid to the last minute you wouldn't. Look at you. Please, please, come. So good to see you."

"Hello, Noriko."

"Close that door and give me a hug."

She held out her thin arms, wrinkled and freckled. I closed the door, set down the sword and the bag of sake and hugged her bony body. She had recently been in the bath. When I stood back, she raked her hands down the front of her blouse. "I'll bet you did not expect to see me like this, did you?"

I shook my head. "I admit it was a surprise."

"Multiple sclerosis. Karma, neh? She said, cheerily. "Lucky it's in remission; I can walk short distances but with great difficulty. Well," she said, looking me up and down. "I can see you've brought the sword. That wasn't necessary, but my family will be very grateful, although there are very few remaining members alive. Besides, no one cares about old things anymore."

I heard this but it really didn't register that she was telling me, really and truly, that the sword didn't matter.

A cat meandered in front hallway and jumped up on her lap. "Miro," she said, "meet my old friend, Noppo."

Miro ignored me. Noriko pushed the cat off her lap.

She looked up and grabbed my hand. "Oh, so good to see you, Noppo. Come now, let's sit down at the breakfast table so we can have a proper talk."

I took off my shoes. She watched me then turned and wheeled herself around. I shuffled behind her in my stocking feet carrying the sword and the bag that contained the bottle of sake. I was surprised at how at ease I felt.

"I don't recall you being much of a breakfast person, Noriko. Have you developed a morning appetite with age?"

She shook her head without looking at me. "Eat like a sparrow in the morning. Eat like a sparrow most of the time actually. Not like the old days. Mostly tea and sometimes little misoshiru. That's it."

"And you cook for yourself?"

"What?" She turned and looked at me but did not stop wheeling herself, and grinned. "Noriko having to attend to domestic chores herself? Don't be so daft, Noppo. I have a full-time cook and housekeeper and assistant."

"It's not Atsuko, is it?"

"No, although Atsuko was with me until about ten years ago. My complications with MS became too much for her. She was old and weak. She continued to live with me but she became jealous of the new maid. She kept wanting to serve. Three women under the same roof? Not recommended, Noppo."

"Your new cook couldn't have been that happy to get up so early."

"She has grown accustomed to demands at odd hours. Such is the fate of working for eccentric old Noriko."

A corner of a living room has been converted into a dining area. The house was a combination of new and old, mostly old. I looked up at the ceiling. The ancient beams probably had no nails. White plaster walls with dull brown beams placed at irregular intervals. They were hand pegged and I guessed this place must be at least 300 years old. The dark wood floor gleamed from polish. No tatami mats, which I presumed was due to Noriko's travelling about in a wheelchair. One south-facing window with small panes overlooked a small garden. A western-style table, set for two, sat in the corner.

Quiet cooking noises came from the kitchen. I smelled steamed rice.

Noriko turned and gestured towards western style chair at one end of the table. "Come. Sit down, please."

I didn't sit but gave her the bottle of sake. "For old time's sake and for consumption at some other time."

"What's the matter with right now?" she asked.

"It's a little early in the morning for that, don't you think?"

She looked up at me. "When is the next time we shall see each other? Fifty-one years has passed since we saw each other last. What a pair of old sticks we are," she said, laughing.

"I see your grasp of the English language hasn't diminished any," I said, sitting.

"Well, thank you, Noppo. When I got married, I quit my job at NHK but quickly become very bored just being a housewife with children."

She made a face like motherhood disagreed with her. "I took a part time job as a speech coach. Fancy that. Actors. Politicians. Corporate titans that wanted to sound like Englishmen. They showed up at my door. They paid me handsomely and it allowed me to keep up with my English. Several times, after my children were older and before MS attacked my body, I was paid to lead tours of England."

"How old were you when MS arrived?"

"Sixty-one. An outlier in every epidemiological sense."

"You seem to be managing all right."

"Yes, yes, Noppo," she said a little impatiently. "I don't want to spend the precious time we have together talking about my disease. How long can you stay?"

"A few hours. I fly out this afternoon."

Noticing an absence of ashtrays, I asked: "No Lucky Strikes?"

"Oh, I would adore one, but the doctors say it aggravates my MS. You didn't by chance bring any cigarettes, did you? My daughter would kill me but she won't be here until early afternoon. You look so well, Noppo. You haven't changed a bit."

I rubbed the top of my head. "My hair has gotten a bit thinner and grayer since you saw me last?"

"Just barely. Now, where should we start?"

She turned her head towards the kitchen. "Kasumi," she said in Japanese. "Bring the green tea."

A middle-aged woman entered carrying a tray. She stopped briefly, bowed, then set the tray on the table. She bowed again. Noriko gave her the bottle of sake. "Please heat to a proper temperature."

Kasumi bowed, said *hai,* as if it was normal to sip sake at 6:15 in the morning, took the bottle and left.

I had placed the sword on a side table. I touched it with my hand. I wanted to get this part over with. "Would you like to hear what happened with this?"

She sighed impatiently, but then said sympathetically. "If you must, Noppo, but I'd rather we talk about something else. If you must know, the sword was the least of our problems, although it did create tension when my family discovered it was gone. Besides, I did not tell them right away."

"How long did you wait before saying something?"

"Oh, at least a year," she said with a shrug.

I was stunned. Finally, I said, "A year? Why? Weren't you furious with me for taking it?"

"No. I was relieved. I felt so guilty for what had happened. Please, Noppo. Don't get the wrong idea. I am very grateful you returned the sword. This has been bothering you for a long time, hasn't it?"

I had a whole speech planned. But she truly wasn't interested. All this time I was burdened with the projection that the sword's theft had caused great shame. What a waste of energy. Noriko: ever unpredictable.

"I did not tell my parents it was you," she said, "although I knew you were the culprit. I just told them a thief broke into my apartment when I was gone and discovered the sword's hiding place. Taki and my mother were very upset. The sword was from her side of the family."

I nodded and wanted move past my foolish disappointment. "So, how about we start when you stopped answering my telephone calls and your desk at NHK sat unoccupied?"

"*So desu nee*. Of course. Here, let me pour you some tea before it gets too strong."

She filled the two cups with light jade-colored liquid and set the pot down on the tray. She handed me a cup, her hands trembling slightly. Noriko took a sip and nodded her approval of the flavor. She held the cup in her hands, as if to warm her joints. "Noppo, our relationship set off a seismic shock wave in my family from which we never fully recovered. What's the old English idiom? Upset the apple cart?"

She paused and sighed.

I said, "I remember that visit to your apartment before the trip to Hawaii. You and Taki had been fighting on the telephone. It seemed to me that it went downhill from there. Was I right?"

"With the speed of Galileo's cannonballs falling from the tower," she confirmed, employing an unexpected metaphor. Then she corrected herself. "Well, maybe not that fast, but close."

"What did happen? You never fully explained."

"Fully explain? Oh, dear," she said, as just the thought of going into the details wearied her. "My mother," she said, as if that would clarify everything.

"What about her? I know she was not pleased that you were with me."

"That's an understatement. Our relationship infuriated her. She couldn't believe my insolence. Obedience and hierarchy had been violated. Do you know, Noppo, that one of my first memories is mother pushing my head down when I did not bow fast enough to an uncle who I'd only seen once before?"

Noriko moved her jaw around a bit in contemplation. "My mother never recovered from the war. The defeat of Japan struck a fatal blow to her psyche. The occupation, for her, was a nightmare. You know that. But as the relationship between you and me progressed, her projected world collapsed and she went a little loopy. Actually, not just a little. She eventually went full on starkers. She developed all sorts of phobias, mostly of the outside world. She stopped going out of the house, which didn't bother me much, but she also insisted that not only was I forbidden to marry a gaijin but I must never intimately associate with someone who had taken part in defeating Japan."

Noriko shook her head, still regretting her mother's behavior. "This became her obsession, Noppo. She went as far as telling me that if I ever brought you home, I would never be allowed to pass through their door again."

"Sounds awful," I said. "Why didn't you say something? Did this happen after I met them at Rikugien Garden?"

She paused, thinking, and wobbled her head a bit. "It's been so long ago I can't remember. No. You are right. It was the trip to Hawaii that tipped her over the edge."

"But you went to Honolulu anyway?

"Yes, I did. Are you sure you didn't bring any cigarettes?"

"No, but would you like me to go buy some?"

She waved her hand. "You haven't changed, have you, Noppo? Still the unbearably nice chap. No, no. Never mind the cigarettes. Too far away and it would take too much time away from our conversation."

"What happened after Hawaii? You began drifting away."

"Hawaii. Yes," she turned her chair and began speaking if she was addressing someone out the window. "Honolulu seems centuries ago. I did, didn't I? Drifting, yes," she said in a faraway voice. "It's one thing to lose your moorings, Noppo. It's another thing to not recognize you've lost your mooring until you're adrift far out to sea. You wake up one day and you can see nothing but ocean. I'm sure you could see I was on the outs with my family, my mother especially. I was sick of my spineless father and my brilliant but manipulative brother and their bloody sense of propriety. I was ready to give the whole lot of them the heave-ho. Very un-Japanese, I know. And the unbearable condescension I had to suffer at NHK."

"Condescension? Was it that bad? I recall you seemed pleased for the job you did holding your own at NHK," I said. "And for getting the position in the first place."

She turned the chair towards me and regarded me in silence. "Taki got me that job. They owed him favors. Then they found out I was an asset, that I was a competent and clever editor. That discovery created excruciating tension. For a woman to take over a job traditionally held by a man and do such a superior job. I made many enemies just for being a woman and not giving up. However, my pride continued to seduce me that I had scored a victory for myself."

"Then," she said with a sigh, wheeling the chair back in front the table. "You came along. My savior. The person who would take me away from all of that. I used to thank the gods on a daily basis I had found you. And yet," she paused and fiddled with a pair of chopsticks, "as the months passed I soon found myself torn to pieces. Conflicted. Tangled up in *giri.* So tangled. I hated my family and yet the idea of leaving them and living 6,000 miles across the ocean. Oh. That was too much. I knew they'd never come to see me. I'd have to fly back to Japan and see them. So tangled," she repeated.

"And," she said, taking another sip of tea. "It got even more complicated than a seriously dotty mother, if you can imagine that. My father actually grew a bit of a spine. Finally. An English spine, if you like. He told me that I must live my own life, not the life that was expected of me. If I wanted to marry you, he would support me, including financially, even if I moved to the United States, which of course I would have if I married you. Somehow my mother got wind of this conversation. She moved out of the bedroom. For a very traditional Japanese woman to do that is terribly serious situation. She never let me forget for a moment I was the cause of all this."

"And Taki?"

She gripped both sides of the chair bowed her head and held it down for a good ten seconds. "O, Noppo. That was the worst. I loved and admired my brother, even though he could be a stuffed shirt and impossible. He was more complicated than me, if that's possible. I so valued his opinion and approval. He was trying to be the good filial son and honor the intentions of his father. But in here," Noriko made a fist and gently thumped her chest, "he was connected to my mother. He began refusing to talk to me. Oh that hurt. Unbearably."

She stared at me then said, "you must be very hungry, Noppo. Let's eat some breakfast."

I wasn't in the mood for food, but could tell from the smells coming from the kitchen that breakfast was in the making.

Noriko turned towards the kitchen. "Kasumi. Breakfast, please. And sake."

She turned back to me, her face melancholy, and looked right through me.

"One day – I remember this very clearly – I was riding the trolley into work. I looked out the window and I saw a GI walking down the street arm and arm with a Japanese woman. I realized I could not live with the choices before me. I thought my heart would literally burst from grief if I lost you. But to totally abandon my family. I owed too much. My rebellion could go just so far. I began crying, weeping very hard, uncontrollably, while sitting in my trolley seat."

Noriko's eyes became damp. She reached for my hand. "So, my darling Noppo. I had to let you go. Do you remember the last time we saw each other?"

"Of course. At Mrs. Ogawa's. You looked very pale and lost weight you couldn't afford to lose. You barely touched your sake."

"I had simply given up eating, Noppo. I was thinking about suicide. Death means release from conflict, release from all obligation. It seemed the only way out. I think it was the day after that I gave notice for a leave of absence at NHK. I went home and had Atsuko pack our bags. I went to stay with my sister. It was the safest place. You did not know where she lived."

"I tried to find her," I said.

"Yes. I suspected you would. But she lived a long ways way. Hokkaido. I stayed with her family for almost three months."

"I kept running past your apartment, hoping I would see you or Atsuko. Never did."

She nodded. "I knew the day your commission expired and I waited until it had passed before returning. I was confident you would leave Japan promptly. Was I right?"

"You were."

"Well, I thought my life did not get any easier when I returned. It didn't. I was demoted at NHK, practically a secretary. They wanted to fire me but of course they wouldn't. I thought family matters might return to some degree of stability but they did not," she said.

Noriko dropped her head "Oh," she said, shaking it, then looked up. "Shibusawa Trading managed to stay afloat but Matataka Chemical could not survive in modern Japan. It filed for bankruptcy. Taki was chairman and could not take the shame. He hung himself. I met my future husband at his funeral. So strange, neh?"

I had a macabre vision of Taki dressed in one of his Saville Row suits hanging from a rope.

Noriko wanted to change the subject and in a scolding tone called out to Kasumi, asking what was keeping her from serving us.

The food and sake arrived. Kasumi set a small bowl of miso shiro in front of Noriko. In my place, she set a plate of *umaki*: slices of eel wrapped in tamagoyaki or Japanese omelet. Noriko grinned. "You still like, unagi, big boy?"

"I do and I don't think I've had this since I left Japan."

"Well, good. Memory food. Tuck in, Noppo."

Kasumi poured the sake in plain ceramic cups, first me then Noriko. She bowed then left. Noriko lifted up her cup and employed the classic British salutation. "Cheers, Noppo. Now, what about you? You married. Children?"

I told her of my two marriages and children. Then she asked me about work. When I told her about being a Japanese risk and political analyst for almost 50 years, she said I must have occasionally returned to Japan.

"Oh, yes. Many times. Mostly in Tokyo, however."

"And you never thought to come see me?" She seemed surprised if not a little wounded.

"Thought, Noriko? You have no idea how many times I ran that scenario through my brain. What would have that accomplished? I was afraid if I ever saw you again, I would be overcome with both love and grief and I would relive the whole ordeal all over again. Too painful."

"Yes, of course," said Noriko, almost chastising herself. "Of course. Best to stay away. Although I would have welcomed a visit. There is something else I must tell you, Noppo."

"What's that?

She thumbed the edge of her soup bowl. "I left because you were too good for me."

I thought my hearing aids had failed me. "Noriko. How is that possible? The son of an untenured teacher at a two-year state college?"

"Noppo," she said gravely. "Don't be silly. That's not what I mean."

"I knew," she said, "I knew you were looking into my family's past. NHK had a mole in SCAP and he told me you were on the hunt for information about Shibuzawa Trading. I also knew, given your intelligence and persistence, that you would find out about Mataka Trading. Although I'm deeply ashamed of my family's background – profiting from poisons – it is also who I am. I cannot escape it as much as I'd like to. You, Noppo, while you did not come from the dirt poor, you came from people who made their living associating with people of the soil. You, on your own talent, sheer talent, rose to a very elevated position. You probably do not know this but for a while, NHK considered you one of the most important people in Japan."

"Oh, come now, Noriko. I was just a lackey who spoke decent Japanese."

She shook her head vigorously and wagged her finger at me. "No, no. Don't be so self-deprecating. Don't be so *Japanese*," she grinned. "Your fluency and understanding of the Japanese people, connected with your access to MacArthur, made you very important. You had a lot to be proud of and no ghosts in the closet."

She sat up in her chair and pointed towards herself. "For me, and for my family, we suffered the curse of aristocracy: ghosts lurking in every corner," she said, sweeping her hand around the room. "Everywhere I turned I bumped into a ghost. It's just the way it is, although if I could blame anyone, it would not be my mother. It would be my father."

She paused and took a sip of sake. "Did you, Noppo, ever read that book? Oh, what it's called? Yes. *Onna Daigaku*, written in the Tokugawa era, about how women should act?"

I shook my head.

"I'm surprised. You and your knowledge of Japanese literature. My mother gave me a copy when I was young girl. There was section where the author says that a parent should not raise their daughter with excess tenderness because she will grow up self-willed and capricious. My father was very indulgent with me. When I look back at myself when you and I shared a bed, I can see what a difficult person I was, completely incapable of self-inspection or self-reflection. And the fact is I'm really no different, now, Noppo."

"And how did how your eventual husband handle you?" Out of my mouth before I knew it.

Noriko regarded me with a wry smile. "It was simple, really. I ended up marrying the funeral director's son."

"Tomonosuke? Wasn't he a descendent to a viscount?"

"The viscount died broke, Noppo, stone cold broke. All the heirs got was the status of a name. My husband's family ended up in a business that turned out to be quite lucrative. That's because no one else wanted to do it. The Japanese turn their noses up at having to deal with the dead. Not as bad as the *eta*, but not so far removed, either. But the security of money was never an issue for me. You know that. I needed a man from lower stock. What was important was that my husband came with imperfections, like me, and we could live in relative harmony as two imperfect people."

The thought of a granddaughter of a *genro* marrying one who tends to the dead seemed so improbable. "Oh, Noriko. What gave you this idea I was perfect? What made you think I thought of myself as such?"

She reached out a grabbed my hand again and squeezed it. "It wasn't as if you didn't have humility, Noppo. It was your expectations of me. I watched you not smoke, keep yourself fit running all over Tokyo, be honest, bury your anger and impatience with me, serve your country – such dedication to your job – and above all, try to see something from someone's else point of view. So noble. I knew you wearied of my quirky actions but I think you felt that if I could just improve myself, I could move to the United States and magically blend in and, at the same time, uphold a standard of behavior that would never match yours. I felt your love would always be conditional. But I loved you, Noppo, so, so much. And I felt your sweet love for me. But it was too much. I felt I didn't deserve it. That's what broke my heart that between my giri and your expectations, that it was a relationship that could never be."

How had I ever thought this relationship would work? And why had I held on to idea that, if only for a few minor differences, Noriko and I could have had a life together?

She poured the sake. First me, then, breaking etiquette, for herself. "But remember, Noppo. This is Japan, where the best love stories have unhappy endings."

###

When I left her house, the rain had stopped. It felt intoxicating to walk through century-old streets of Japan carrying no sword and no gift to an old lover. I felt intensely unencumbered, even liberated, not a feeling common among octogenarians. I was indeed tipsy and had a stash of yen in my pocket. It was like being a young soldier on leave.

For the first time in 50 years, I slept on an airplane. It helped that unlike my packed flight to Osaka, the flight to Honolulu was only half full. After a few hours in the air, I struck up a conversation with a gracefully aging stewardess from Kobe; she was of an age that never would have appeared on a JAL flight when I used to fly the airline for business. The Japanese must be relaxing their fixation with young women. The top deck of the 747 was practically deserted, she said. "Why don't you go up there and lie down on a row of empty seats? Come, I will help you."

I obliged. She found a row, helped me take off my shoes, gave me two pillows then covered me with a blanket. I will wake you 20 minutes before landing."*ii yume wo miru you ni,"* she said. "May you have sweet dreams."

Dreams indeed. The rumble of the Rolls Royce engines lured me to a spot I had not been since I was a child: Craters of the Moon, a basaltic lava field of the Snake River Plain. It is a place of terrible beauty, thousands of acres of gray and black basaltic lava, some smooth a glass, some churned up and spikey as if plagued with an unimaginable skin disease. On the paths, the ground growls under your feet as you walk, crunching thousands of black friable cinders. All of this overseen by the magnificent Pioneer mountains, which, in my dream, were capped with snow.

My father cherished Craters of the Moon and took Peter and me there several times. He had an ancient carbide miner's lamp and led us down into lava tube caves. What he loved most was showing us the plant community that grew in such inhospitable land. Over 600 species live out there, even ferns if you looked in the right places.

My father was in the dream, looking about 35. Noriko and Peter were there also, each in their mid-twenties. The sky was as blue as only it can be in those basins between Rocky Mountain ranges. There was no talking.

All I remembered upon waking was: my world was divided no more.

Sylvia was waiting for me outside of customs holding a lei of fresh jasmine in her hands. She was very tan. Her dermatologist would give her hell. She put the flowers around my neck then looked up and kissed me on the mouth.

"It is so good to see you, Teddy," she said, "without anything in your hands."

www.ingramcontent.com/pod-product-compliance
Lightning Source LLC
LaVergne TN
LVHW061046070526
838201LV00074B/5193